For Barbara.

September 1952.

THE PORTLY PEREGRINE

THE
PORTLY PEREGRINE

by

PETER TRAILL

HERBERT JENKINS LIMITED
3 DUKE OF YORK STREET, ST. JAMES'S,
LONDON, S.W.I

A
HERBERT
JENKINS
BOOK

First printing

MADE AND PRINTED IN GREAT BRITAIN BY PURNELL AND SONS, LTD.,
PAULTON (SOMERSET) AND LONDON

THE
PORTLY PEREGRINE

SOME forty years ago when Mr. Prentice had been a
boy at a preparatory school his headmaster had written
at the end of his final term's report in the space reserved
for his remarks, "He is a nice boy, but has been a difficult
one to teach because of his self-consciousness. He is a weak
classic, but something of a philosopher. I wish him luck."
Mr. Prentice had immediately taken the adjective "nice"
to his bosom as it were and, acknowledging that the rest of
the report was very fair, had been a little touched by the
bestowal of the wish for good fortune. Encouraged by that
and hampered by his diffidence he had taken himself to the
Bar, on the Chancery side of which he had practised with
varying success for a longer time than he cared to admit.

With the help of an efficient clerk and application he
had gained a reputation with many solicitors as a good
draftsman, but a bad advocate, and he made a fair income—
as much as many other barristers whose names were much
more familiar to the public. For this he had had to work
very hard and, though he kept abreast of his expenses, his
income never exceeded them by more than a modest amount.

He had, then, not saved very much, but as his tastes were
simple it was a long time since he had not been in a position
to fulfil them and, though with advancing years he had not
the same affection for the English winter and wished that he
could afford to buy a little sun and, perhaps, work a little less,
he was neither on the verge of senile decay nor a nervous
breakdown. But as he was tired he walked along the sparsely-
filled pavements with slow steps and bent shoulders.

No one could have called Mr. Prentice good-looking and,
indeed, he would have been very much embarrassed had he

known that he had been noticed at all. He had no wish to call attention to himself, and it was certain that no one of the passers-by gave a second thought to the small man who walked quietly along in his black coat and striped trousers; a grey homburg, dirtied by many winters, upon his head and a cherry-stick in his hand. Modestly he walked on the innermost edge of the pavement beneath the shadow of the tall buildings, glancing eagerly every now and then for the name of each fresh turning that debouched from the highway. He was looking for a particular vein where he had been instructed by the house agents to leave the artery and, following the trickle, to find a place called St. Anne's Court. In his right hand he held a key, attached to which was a label bearing, in addition to the name of the Court, the number 6 upon it, and Mr. Prentice was eager to have a look at the house because the lease of his present abode in the Temple was due to expire on the next quarter day and he had as yet nowhere to live.

Mr. Prentice had often thought about the unfortunate people who had nowhere to live; he had put his hand into his pocket for them but, secure in his niche in the Temple, he had never thought that he might be in a somewhat similar position. There was, of course, a radical difference between himself and the unfortunates because he could always find the price of a bed and could do the same for his servant, Markham, and his dog, Lottie Spate, but strange resting places frightened him.

It was his own fault that he was in his present predicament; he had had plenty of time to face the situation, but he had been so busy trying not to face it that now the avalanche was nearly upon him. He had not been able to realize that his flat in the Temple was regarded by the landlords as an anachronism, and they intended not only to redecorate it, but to knock the wall down between it and the adjoining flat to make what they called a "commodious abode"; and since he had realized it he had been in the hands of house agents.

Trusting himself to them he had spent a great deal of his time on fruitless quests for, disregarding his injunctions, they had sent him to inspect properties whose rents were well above the figure he had stipulated, or whose position had nothing in common with his tastes.

At first, he had been so upset by his encounters with caretakers, hall porters and occupiers that he had either left without viewing the places properly or, staying, had nearly agreed to take the tenancy rather than bring himself to say no. But a growing familiarity with adventure had bred a certain independence, and a growing belief that he was never likely to find anything suitable had engendered a kindly resignation.

"The trouble is," he murmured to himself as he walked along, "that I shall never even be allowed a glimpse of the place. As for my chances of taking it I am plainly no Sir Galahad." Indeed, there was no resemblance between the artist's idea of the pure and gallant knight and the stocky and rotund figure of Mr. Prentice, but then neither was there one between the Holy Grail and a suitable house. It was only to the difficulty of the search that he made allusion as his round face grew a little red and damp with the unaccustomed exercise.

Mr. Prentice liked London and, while he endured disappointment, he was conscious all the time of a solid wall of satisfaction that he had been born in the city of the planes, and that his errand, fruitless so far, at any rate enabled him to test the strength of the ties which bound him to it. In his short black coat and striped trousers he felt that he was one of its men, just as when the century was in swaddling clothes and he had roller-skated down its broad pavements in Holland Park he had known that he was one of its children.

Removing his homburg and passing his hand over his forehead he was surprised to find that it was wet. Taking out a clean linen handkerchief he wiped the bald patch whence his dark greying hair had receded, leaving a few strands that had so far escaped disaster as at the ebb a bunch of seaweed remains in the surrounding sand. Then he grasped his stick firmly again and continued on his quest, the sky grey above him and the street becoming more crowded as the shops put up their shutters and released their workers.

Suddenly his step became livelier and, in spite of his paunch and the shortness of his stride, he went faster than the majority of those who were hurrying for their buses or trains. His brown eyes had read the name of the turning which he had been told to take and, leaving the thoroughfare, he went down the by-road eagerly. Half-way along it he came to a narrow opening, drawn across which was a long, shining and expensive motor car. High up in the archway he read "St. Anne's Court" and, skirting the car with difficulty, went in beneath the arch and stood looking about him.

The time was a little before seven o'clock early in September when it is popularly supposed that London is empty. The quiet about him aided the popular idea, for not a sound was to be heard in or around the courtyard in which he stood except the distant hum of the traffic. Mr. Prentice moved cautiously forward and, coming to the centre of the rectangle, examined the bole of an ash tree. The lower branches of the tree had been cut away and their origins sealed, but high above him their lofty fellows stirred gently in the breeze above the roofs of the houses. There were six of these, three on one side of the paved courtyard and three on the other. They were upon two floors with no basements, and all had latticed windows. At the foot of those on the ground floor there were small beds of flowers, stocks with an edging of catmint, and Mr. Prentice, who knew little about horticulture, thought the scene charming and the faint scent enticing. But most of all he thought about peace.

Fingering the lapel of his coat in uncertain fashion and grasping the key firmly in his other hand, he crossed over to the nearest doorway with the idea of discovering the arithmetic progression of the numbers. For some time he looked at the figure I in wrought iron on the centre panel of the oak door, conscious of the iron lantern suspended above his head and aware of the blue curtains that hung straight and motionless behind the diamond-leaded panes of the windows on either side of him. Then suddenly aware that he was guilty of vulgar curiosity he coughed deprecatingly to himself and, moving hastily away, walked precipitously across the courtyard to the further corner where he judged that number

6 lay. It was then that he saw the marigolds and noticed that while all the other gardens were uniform, the one in the front of number 6 was edged with bachelor's buttons instead of catmint, and marigolds splashed their gold where stocks grew in the others. The sight made Mr. Prentice feel gay and, holding the label in his hand, he twirled the key round and round, humming to himself a few bars of that lively march, Lorraine. Then, as a general, newly appointed, is eager to make himself acquainted with the area of his command, so he stepped forward with alacrity and, placing the key in the lock, threw open the door.

No Aladdin's cave confronted him. Mr. Prentice, with all his hopes that one day he might be privileged as St. Thomas to see a miracle performed, had not expected such an easy way of paying the premium and the rent of the house to be forthcoming; but he was a little subdued by the bare boards of the hall. The sturdy march died away upon his lips and he advanced, not in the manner of a general with his baton truculent, but as a corporal in charge of a wiring party, wary and ready for any surprise. Before him the stairs led upwards, but Mr. Prentice deemed it prudent to reconnoitre the ground floor first. On his left and on his right the blank faces of the shut doors confronted him. He chose the left and was enveloped in a murky twilight which was due to the dirt on the diamond panes of the windows. On the further side he saw a hatch in the wall and, having decided that he stood in the dining-room, he turned his back on it immediately. Dining-rooms did not interest him. Opening the door on the right he entered a room of similar size, but one wall of this was lined with bookshelves and there were the ashes of a fire in the grate.

These two sights heartened him, for where there were bookshelves there had been books, and where there were ashes had been a fire. Encouraged by this knowledge he turned on the light on the dark staircase and, going upstairs to have a look at the two bedrooms and bathroom which his printed slip of paper told him he would find, surveyed their bare interiors with confidence. He had a liking for wallpapers, not the plain kind with a frieze that was nearly out of sight, but the cheerful sort, and he remembered one that had been covered with bunches of cherries. But that was when he was a boy and cherries had never seemed to be so red since those days; he remembered another with forget-me-nots tied in small bunches down its length; he remembered yet a third with a pattern of purple irises, but that had been a trifle over-whelming. The three wallpapers represented three milestones in his life in the days when money and responsibility were mysterious things which worried the grown-up world, but not boys like himself. Indeed, he had not understood why the conversation of grown-up people appeared to be almost entirely devoted to one or the other. If he asked his mother for a penny it was forthcoming and there were no problems which could not be settled by just leaving them alone and beginning on something fresh. But he had not forgotten that the houses grew smaller and, where the purple irises flowered in such profusion on his wall, there were none in the mean streets outside whereas once they had had red cherries from their own trees and later, though they had no fruit, the forget-me-nots had lined the flower beds in front of their house.

There was no wallpaper on the walls of the little house in St. Anne's Court. Mr. Prentice put his fingers gingerly upon the surface and sighed. He recognized the feel of his old enemy, washable distemper; but he bore no malice. The rancour in his heart at the flat uniform colours had long since abated and, after all, he still had his coal fire in his study.

Mr. Prentice was not hard of hearing, but he didn't always listen; and nothing subdues the present as memories of the past. He was back there with his cherries when he felt, without seeing, the presence of someone else in the room. Turning in vague apprehension he found a little girl standing in the doorway. She stood shyly mostly upon one foot and, sucking her thumb, regarded him with her steady blue eyes. Mr. Prentice was embarrassed and, in the silence, tried to think what the boy with his cherries would have said. He would, he felt, have been able at any rate to meet, and perhaps to master, the situation. But one of the troubles about age is that one forgets so much in attaining it and while Mr. Prentice could deal, not with a great show of confidence, with those who had travelled down the road of life, he had completely forgotten how to shake hands with those upon the threshold. Desperately he tried to remember how his mother had treated him and his young friends, but of all the things that she had said he could not recall one that was apposite.

"I thought you were Iris," the little girl said suddenly; at least that was what Mr. Prentice imagined she said, but as she still kept her thumb in her mouth he was not altogether certain. He noted, however, her clean blue dress, her white socks and her neat shoes with satisfaction and, having hastily dropped his eyes when he had found hers so gravely fixed on them, raised them at the sound of her voice and saw that her face was delicate. Her fair hair, carefully brushed and curling beyond her ears, made her features look tiny; but her head sat squarely upon her narrow shoulders and she regarded him without fear.

"No," he answered. "I'm not Iris."

The little girl considered the statement; then she took her thumb from her mouth and came a little nearer to him.

"Iris said she would come back," she announced and Mr. Prentice felt the weight of her disapproval for him.

"Perhaps she will," he said hopefully.

"She said she would."

"Nothing is certain," Mr. Prentice informed her quickly, since it seemed disastrous to him that the child should nail her faith so obstinately to the mast. He had always tried to keep an open mind upon all questions, however simple and obvious the answers might appear. The little girl disregarded his well-meant advice.

"What are you doing here?" she asked.

Mr. Prentice felt the reproach in her tone and, his thoughts busy with the truth or untruth of his own statement, scratched his head.

"I'm thinking of living here," he answered at length, conscious that the announcement would not be received favourably and hardly daring to meet the little girl's eyes which, he told himself, were as blue as the skies in the Pyrenees.

"You can't do that," she replied with decision. "It belongs to Iris."

Mr. Prentice started to put his hat back on his head, then dropping his hand to his side again, regarded the toecaps of his worn, but well polished, black shoes.

"It doesn't," he said miserably. "It belongs to the Earl of Rawton. Iris must have been a leaseholder and either her lease has lapsed or she forfeited it." He looked at her again. "Frankly, I think, it is the former which——"

"She isn't coming back," the little girl broke in and her eyes suddenly became moist.

Mr. Prentice started towards her in dismay.

"Nothing is certain," he reiterated hastily. "That's the great thing about life, you know. I expect you've found it out already," he rushed on. "It took me a long time, much longer, I think, than it's taken you. If you knew beforehand exactly what was going to happen there would be no excitement."

The little girl continued to look at him forlornly and Mr. Prentice made desperate efforts to steer the conversation into a channel which would, he hoped, be familiar to her.

"Take your name, for instance," he continued. "It might be Beryl, Gladys, Rose or June or—almost anything. If I knew it beforehand that would have taken away some of the charm of our meeting."

The little girl tossed her head and the fair curls shivered.

"It's Paula," she said.

"I should never have guessed it," Mr. Prentice answered truthfully.

"I live at the house at the end," she went on, pointing vaguely towards the window.

"The one with the blue curtains?" he asked, his voice displaying more confidence than heretofore.

Paula nodded.

"Have you got a wife or anything?" she asked.

Mr. Prentice judged that she was taking an intelligent interest in him for the first time since their encounter and he felt flattered.

"I don't think I'm the sort of man that women want to marry," he confided in her. "But I've got a dog and a man-servant."

Paula pursed her lips together and a frown spread over her small forehead.

"I haven't seen one of those," she acknowledged frankly.

Mr. Prentice assumed that she was referring to Mr. Markham and not to Lottie Spate which was the name of his spaniel.

"You'll like Mr. Markham," he said.

"Will you be staying here long?" she countered.

"That depends."

"Nothing is certain, is it?" she announced.

Mr. Prentice bowed very slightly in acknowledgment of a lesson truly learnt. Whether Paula took this to mean that the interview was closed, or whether she had become tired of the conversation, she suddenly turned on her heels and, running from the room, hurried down the uncarpeted stairs.

That was the way to take one's leave. How much better it was, Mr. Prentice reflected, as he listened to the sound of her shoes gradually diminishing, to abandon a conversational position the moment it became irksome than to engage in the mumbo-jumbo of conventional excuses, and now that she had gone he could think of no cogent reason why he should prolong his own stay.

Following her down the stairs he arrived again at the front door where, after he had closed it behind him, he stood for a moment and looked out upon a smooth courtyard. There was no sign of Paula, nor of anyone else, and the scent of the stocks softly enfolded him. Mr. Prentice had always championed the cause of flowers in London, though he was un-enthusiastic about the geraniums which generally represented the height of achievement to those who thought as he did, but while the perfume wooed him he kept his eyes upon the marigolds. A sparrow twittered a moment in the tall ash tree and, as he walked slowly over the flagstones towards the archway, he noted once more the blue curtains; but he did not notice that the large and expensive car was no longer drawn across the entrance to the Court.

As he made his way back to the busy thoroughfare Mr. Prentice appeared to be doing that impossible thing, adding a cubit to his stature. The little round paunch was not so protuberant, the bowed shoulders were straight, the homburg sat jauntily on the dark grey-dappled hair above his ears and the ferrule of his cherry-stick struck the pavement with a sharp insistent note, like the tap of a kettle drummer who keeps the step tidy while the rest of the band takes its ease. He was overjoyed that he was no longer to be homeless in the vast city for, though the premium would run away with a large part of his savings, he was determined to live in number 6, St. Anne's Court; and he reflected that, after all, the house agents had not been so stupid as they appeared to be. Every man is supposed to have his price and they had found out his. He had arrived, he had seen and he had been conquered, and the financial rules by which his existence had been governed were to be waived. The circumstances, he argued to himself, warranted it and, furthermore, contentment could not be measured in pounds, shillings and pence. A man should pay for a thing what he deemed it worth, and Mr. Prentice was willing to give a hostage to fortune.

He waited for his bus patiently. As a rule when he did this he spent his time observing his fellow citizens, wondering at their patience and good humour and trying to solve the riddle of their lives as they stood, leaning out over the kerbstones and watching the numbers of the buses with the same concentration as a roulette player broods over the flying wheel. But this evening he paid no attention to them; he thought only of getting himself and his possessions safely housed before the end of the year.

Like his forebears he was making things safe against the winter when the wild dogs, or the wolves, would ravage the supplies which were not already in the larder. But his bacon was safely housed unless—and an apprehensive shiver caused him to shed the added cubit—there were terms in the lease which should prove too onerous. He had small confidence in the legal instrument which he had not drawn up himself, and there was little to be wondered at in that because it was from the mistakes of others that he had built up his treasure, such as it was.

The moment he set foot in his flat in the Temple he knew that he had incurred the disapproval of his servant, Markham, who made no attempt to take his hat and stick which was the outward and visible sign of his inward and spiritual displeasure. Mr. Prentice realized at once that he was late. His young red spaniel, however, jumped up at him and eagerly licked his fondling fingers, and her master saw in her actions evidence of the injustice which existed everywhere in the world. The dog gave him a welcome and did not condemn him unheard, but liking him was prepared to be friendly with him at any time, overlooking his shortcomings and making allowances for his faults in the firm belief that, sooner or later, he would see the error of his ways and devote his time entirely to going for walks with bagfuls of bones.

"But then you're a woman, aren't you?" he addressed his dog as he went into the tiny dining-room, "and women have infinite patience," he added without looking at his manservant who stood by the side table, incurious and cold.

The moment Mr. Prentice sat down Markham seized a plate and, advancing to the table in the manner of a person who has a distasteful task to perform, put it down disdainfully in front of him. Returning to the side table where a heater had kept things hot, he advanced again with a dish of cutlets while Mr. Prentice, fondling the long ears of his dog, kept his eyes upon the table. As Markham stood beside him, offering the dish with an air of one who didn't care whether the offer was accepted or not, the manservant looked like a human question mark and melancholy sat enthroned on his long features. It was the presence of this great sadness which had caused Mr. Prentice to engage him for he had found himself from his earliest youth unable to resist sorrow. Into the lap of the tearful goddess he, as a boy, had thrown his marbles, his cigarette pictures and, ultimately, his stamps; in adolescence, his pennies, and at all times his compassion.

When he had interviewed Markham some ten years previously he thought he had never seen sadness so clearly marked. The pale blue eyes that lacked lustre as those of the fool in the forest; the long face which dripped to a lantern jaw; the hollowed cheeks; the small mouth like a miser's purse; the finely spun, sparse and almost colourless fair hair; the meatless body—all cried out for succour; and though he was really in the process of trying to engage a fat and homely general female servant, he had stretched out his hand, meta-phorically speaking, to grasp the bony fingers of Markham. So he had saved him, as he thought, from some sliver of an embankment bench, only to find that his melancholy was a cloak thrown out by his mind. It was an attitude; from what Mr. Prentice could gather from his past and from what had been his present since he had been in his service Markham had certainly experienced little that was heartbreaking.

Though he knew such to be the facts Mr. Prentice, who had a great respect for facts, could not bring himself to believe, confronted daily as he was with such visual evidence, that his manservant was not a very unhappy man. He had come to regard him as a living emblem of the world's misery and retained him as much to preserve himself from any self-satisfaction which he might feel from time to time when the world smiled upon him, as for the more realistic reason that he was afraid to give him notice. Indeed, he viewed himself as another Blackstone upon this matter and relieved his man-servant from the rigours of the Common Law, which insisted on his instant dismissal, by invoking a liberal dose of equity. Allowances, he felt, should be made for a face like Markham's and if he had not, in fact, both feet in the Slough of Despond he should have had them there.

"You appear to have something in common with the hangman," Mr. Prentice remarked, pretending to notice the proffered dish for the first time and taking a cutlet from it. "You deal only in necks."

"That's a cutlet," Markham answered, sighing heavily in the belief that the neck had only one bone. "It's over-cooked, but that is your fault. You like to dine at seven-thirty; others like to dine later. But seven-thirty is seven-thirty and not later." He went away with the dish, and Mr. Prentice, while he waited for his vegetables, began to fondle the dog's ears again.

"It appears that I am guilty of one of your traditional sins," he addressed her. "Women are always accused of being unpunctual. They have a very good reason; they don't like to be kept waiting. Like you they also like attention and a pinch of unpunctuality works wonders. Only a pinch, mind you! Everything has to be measured exactly to be effective."

Markham stood patiently beside him, the vegetable dishes in his hands while Mr. Prentice talked to Lottie Spate, and the moment he paused thrust one of them before him in such a way that his master had the potatoes literally under his nose. Mr. Prentice helped himself in silence but, when Markham had left the table, delivered his news.

"I have found a new roof to our heads which will, I think, suit us admirably," he announced, carefully keeping his eyes upon his plate.

Markham showed no sign of any enthusiasm.

"It is near Holland Park," Mr. Prentice continued.

"Holland Park," Markham repeated in sepulchral tones.

"Do you know the district?" Mr. Prentice asked, picking up his knife and fork and making a *coup de sabre* at the cutlet. At so plain an indication that the evening meal was about to begin Lottie Spate took up her position on her hind legs and watched every movement of her master's hands with bright eyes.

"I've never been so far out," Markham answered, a sharp note of disapproval in his tone.

"It is one of six little houses standing round a courtyard. There is an ash tree in the centre," Mr. Prentice continued, cutting through the meat with difficulty and ignoring Markham's unfriendly attitude.

"The leaves will fall in the gutters and block them," he objected.

"You'll have to unblock them. You can't expect to enjoy anything if you make no contribution yourself," Mr. Prentice said.

"Trees are for the country," Markham answered. "One does not expect to find the Strand in the middle of a wood, or the opposite."

"One would like to," Mr. Prentice said, giving up his

struggle with the cutlet. Taking it gingerly by the bone, he dropped it at the feet of the waiting dog. "So I reward your faith in me," he addressed her. "Besides, you don't mind whether the meat is tough or not."

The dog sank to the carpet and retired under the oak dresser with the bone where she put her jaws round it in earnest.

"There are six houses facing a courtyard," Markham put in, showing no sign that Mr. Prentice's remarks to his dog held any significance for him.

"Ours is number 6," Mr. Prentice answered, eating his vegetables placidly. "I have a weakness for courtyards, or quadrangles, if you prefer it. The Universities thrive on them. No quadrangle, no college. It is part of our system of education. As yet I have never had the fortune to be properly educated."

"Education may be all right for those that like it," Markham said. "And so may quadrangles. But we're best as we are." He looked very sad indeed. "Suppose we don't like the rest of the people in the court. And we shan't."

Mr. Prentice thought of the little girl.

"But we shall," he answered confidently. "Besides, I don't expect we shall see them. We don't see them here."

"Here's different," Markham assured him. "Gates get locked and there's no night life."

"Night life!" Mr. Prentice echoed. "How d'you know? We don't see anyone here because we don't try and we shan't try at St. Anne's Court. Besides, no one will want to see us. Who wants to talk to an old man like me who spends his time routing about in the law reports? But we shall see six little gardens; five of them have stocks in them. But ours has marigolds." He paused and looked at Markham for the first time. One look at the latter's face drove the triumph, which the memory of the marigolds had engendered, out of his own. "Marigolds," he went on soberly, "have always appealed to me. They represent money to me. Real money—sovereigns. I expect the late Doctor Freud would dig up an esoteric reason for the association. But to me it's quite simple. I've never had much money. When I am in St. Anne's Court I shall have less and I am not getting any younger." He pushed his plate away from him. "What I need is a nice fat family trust action with no quarter and an array of silks."

Markham came forward to take his plate and to put the cheese in front of him while Lottie Spate, hastily finishing the rest of the cutlet, appeared again in the guise of a beggar to find out what move might be forthcoming now that the plates had been changed.

"No more for you, Lottie Spate," Mr. Prentice said, and the dog, dropping to her feet, wagged her tail and curvetted about his legs. Mr. Prentice looked at her indulgently.

"You never saw the real Lottie Spate did you, Markham?" he asked. "She was before your time."

"I never go to the theatre," he replied.

"What a mistake you make," Mr. Prentice said, still watching the dog. "You see how she cajoles with her wiggles and her bright eyes. Almost she seems to smile. Just like Lottie Spate used to do. She had auburn hair, too. With her wiggles and her eyes and her smiles she used to get bracelets."

"You knew the woman?" Markham asked sorrowfully.

Mr. Prentice shook his head.

"No," he answered. "I was just a humble admirer. I used to whistle her songs. She was a very beautiful woman—from the gallery," he added. "I still think she is the most beautiful woman I have ever seen—from the gallery."

Markham allowed a smile to spread over his face, but it was so joyless that it was obvious that his master's recollections gave him no pleasure.

"Close up I expect she looked——" he began, but Mr. Prentice held up his knife.

"Cherish your illusions and be thankful," he said. "And remember that no woman would ever have gone to look at us and sigh. The gallery is the place for us. Besides, I've never had the price of a bracelet—I don't know about you."

He got up from his chair and snapped his fingers at the dog who rose to them and licked them, her tail wagging rapidly.

"Lottie Spate's dead and yet she lives. This one prefers cutlets to bracelets, and she's right. As long as one has enough to eat and a roof and preserves one's illusions one can add up correctly the sum of a happy existence."

He moved slowly out of the dining-room, the dog at his heels, while Markham without comment began to clear the table behind him. Crossing the passage he went in to his small study on the floor of which were a number of books; some shut, some open, some small, some large, some bound in half calf and some with their backs off. On the desk lay a mass of papers and tossed aside in the corner sprawled a twisted piece of pink tape.

Sitting down in his swivel chair, he turned on his reading lamp with a green shade and picking up the topmost sheet from the pile of papers began to read the words "To advise on evidence." Putting it aside he began to read systematically through the troubles of the litigants, but after a moment he laid the brief down because he discovered that his mind would not be dragooned in such a fashion. In the interrogatories there was no answer to the apparently trivial question which kept worrying him. Why had Iris left St. Anne's Court?

One Tuesday only a fortnight later Markham rather than Mr. Prentice moved into the new house. Having made up his mind to take Number 6, Mr. Prentice felt that that was as far as he could be expected to exert himself; indeed, that was as far as he had intended to do so. Accordingly he had given his orders to Markham who had secreted about his person tape measures, pencils, bits of paper, string, foot-rules and all the light baggage necessary to ensure that furnishings of one domicile fitted in some fashion into a new one. That he made a tolerably good job of it was due to his own talents as a handy man as much as to the efforts of various "small" men whom he employed on the recommendations of the various charwomen and porters about and around the Temple.

Mr. Prentice left the whole tiresome business alone and fortified himself against the complaints of his manservant by repeating at intervals "*de minimis non curat lex*", as if the aphorism had some power to render Markham spellbound. The reason, however, for his not appearing on the scene of action was not so much his desire to avoid having to answer the thousand and one petty questions which always pop out of workmen's mouths in times like these as to elude the interest of his neighbours. He felt that the blame for any inconvenience that they might suffer and for any temporary nuisance they might have to endure was better laid at Markham's door than his own. He was capable of dealing with any unpleasantness.

Mr. Prentice never imagined that his neighbours, with perhaps the exception of Paula, would be interested in him at all after the noise had abated and the alarums and excursions ceased in the peaceful backwater. He thought he would slip in late on the Tuesday evening when all was over and, by the time his presence actually became known, would have become, if not an elder statesman, at any rate a personage whom his neighbours accepted without contumely or curiosity.

He imagined that he had succeeded in slipping in unnoticed, but he didn't because his coming had been awaited with a curiosity that it scarcely appeared to warrant; and perhaps the centre of it, quite unknown to Mr. Prentice, was situated in the next house where the next evening Mrs. Cumming lay on a sofa that stretched across the sitting-room window and, a cocktail in her hand, scrutinized the painted toenails of her left foot. She was dangling this in the air the better to see it while the rest of her betrousered figure expressed extreme indolence. She had an oval face, the high cheekbones of which were rather more prominent than is usual in Western women and, for all the redness of her lips, her cheeks were pale. Her eyebrows, pencilled in with great care, surmounted a pair of grey eyes that were large and long-lashed and which gave the lie to her attitude of lazy indifference. So, for the matter of that, did her spare little figure, the only part of which that seemed to move aimlessly being her left foot. Across her half-finished martini she looked gravely at her husband.

"What or where are the doldrums?" she asked.

With the help of a standard lamp and a pair of glasses her husband was reading the evening paper; at least, that was what he seemed to be doing. It was opened out in front of his face and his eyes were looking at the leader page, but in fact his thoughts were far away. At his wife's question he pulled them inside his head again with an effort and, lowering his paper a little, peered at her over its top, a tiny frown gathering on his forehead. This wasn't due to any mental effort he was making to answer her question; it was the direct outcome of what he saw.

When they had first married he had found the independent and aloof character of his wife a very attractive combination; indeed, she fascinated not only himself, but most other young men of her acquaintance. This attraction apparently had not lost its power with other young men, but latterly it had suffered a severe set-back so far as he was concerned. In fact, it was only quite recently that he had actually done what he had had a mind to do for some little time and that was to smack her. Several times he had raised his hand behind her back only to let it flutter to his side again to pinch the seams of his trousers with nervous fingers, while a twisted smile struggled fitfully across his pale, sensitive clean-shaven face.

Recently, however, quite recently, her unruffled pose and her attitude of apparent indifference had made him lose his self-control altogether, and he had laid his hand upon her with a force that was all the greater because he had held it in leash for so long. At once he had felt ashamed of himself and any sign of weakness on his wife's part would have brought him, temporarily at any rate, to his knees; but her reactions had been quite different from what he had expected.

His wife had opened her wide grey eyes wider still and, after looking at his hand and then through his head, had walked from the room without giving any sign that she had even felt the blow. Later he had apologized and she had merely told him to pass the toast and not be tiresome; an answer which had caused his hand to itch once more.

Since then she had appeared to have become even more aloof, if it was possible, and he told himself that whatever might be his own faults they were set off in full by his wife's attitude. At the same time, try as he would, and he had been trying very hard of late, to make a case out for himself and to throw the blame for the disaster for which they were heading upon his wife's shoulders, he had to admit that in many ways she was neither the indolent, incapable or insensible person she appeared to be, though she looked as if she was a mixture of all three. It was true that she shopped expensively, but there was a variety about the meals. It was true that there was an uncertainty about their composition, but they were never dull. On the other hand they were rarely on time because his wife never began to cook them until she felt like it and, even if he drew her attention to the time by shouting at her and at last made her go into the kitchen, the meal never arrived any earlier on that account. He had long since made up his mind that at some undefined moment his wife decided when they were going to dine and no cajoling or blustering had any influence on her, whatever her apparent reactions.

These trivial matters and others of the same light weight did amount to a sizeable reason for the marriage not being the great success which it had promised to be, but he knew, better than anyone else, that these blemishes had been turned by him into blots because he wanted to view them through a magnifying glass. That is to say he knew when he was honest with himself; but this he rarely had been lately, and he had only concentrated upon them to prevent himself dwelling on something which was much more onerous and was in no way his wife's fault.

"I should say you were in them," he replied tartly.

"My dear Norman, I'm in a coma—or practically so," she replied, wiggling her toes and taking a sip of her drink. "At the moment I feel just like a stockbroker."

"My dear Joyce, I thank you," her husband imitated her.

"Oh, I wasn't referring to you, dear," Joyce said languidly. "I expect you've had a perfectly palsied day. Unless you've just remained in the state the oil market always appears to be in and played truant."

She ceased to waggle her foot and looked hard at the top of her toes, avoiding the wary light brown eyes of her husband and the antagonism which was plain from the thrust of his thin, pointed chin.

"What state is that?" he asked in a quiet tense voice.

"Quietly irregular," she said, meeting his challenge firmly, but with no malice.

Norman sank back in his chair and, after staring belligerently at her fair short hair for a moment, rustled his paper and put his face behind it.

"As a matter of fact it was strong," he replied at length when he could bear the silence no longer.

Joyce put her leg down again on the sofa and gave his legs, for that was all she could see of him, an unsmiling and enigmatic glance. Then she contemplated her small hands and sighed.

"I wonder whether the salmon will taste of nail polish," she said. "As I've made the mayonnaise of liquid paraffin a good time should be had by all."

Norman rustled his paper again, but he did not appear from behind it.

"I suppose you know the Bellamys are coming at a quarter to eight," he replied. "It's now nearly a quarter past seven and, unless you go and dress, no time's going to be had by anyone."

Joyce gave up the contemplation of her hands.

"I've also made a *bisque d'homard* into which I've dropped a good deal of red pepper," she continued, paying no attention to her husband's outburst. "Have you ever noticed that Jack Bellamy begins to perspire—or should I say sweat? Some men like women to talk like men."

"I don't."

The monosyllables cracked in the air like shots from a rifle.

"I know you don't, dear," Joyce answered sweetly. "Or rather I know you used not to. You preferred women like I am—decorative and so on—unlike Jack's perspiration. I wonder why he does it? Were you at the Ritz when I waved a bottle of Worcester sauce in front of him? It had a very odd effect."

Norman flung his paper down where it collapsed on the floor and glared at his wife as she lay full length on the sofa, holding the glass by the stem between her fingers and looking at it intently as if the drink it contained was some magic potion.

"Will you go and dress?" he shouted, jumping to his feet and standing before her, his hands thrust into his pockets and his eyes hot with exasperation.

"And to finish up with," Joyce went on casually, "we've got sardines on toast." She frowned. "It's rather a fishy evening, isn't it?" Then she smiled and gave him a fleeting glance. "*N'importe*; you can say I thought it was Friday and as they're Catholics——"

"Are they?"

"I haven't the slightest idea," Joyce admitted languidly. "But we shall soon find out, shan't we?" she continued brightly. "Which reminds me I've sent all the fish knives to have the handles mended; they're all loose. I suppose I've let them soak in the hot water or something. You'd better go next door and borrow some from our new neighbour; he passed the window a little time ago, just as he did yesterday, and he looks as if he'd have fish knives and that sort of thing."

"And what does a man look like who'd have fish knives?" Norman opened his monosyllabic barrage again while his hands became fists in his pockets and his lips set in a thin, uncompromising line.

"Well, though he wears the same sort of clothes as you do, they look quite different. He has an air of intelligent respectability——"

"I suppose I'm an unintelligent rake!" Norman burst in.

"Somehow you don't look as if you'd have silver knives and things, unless you'd pinched them. But, of course, you had until I sent them away to the jewellers, which only goes to show——"

"For God's sake go and dress!" Norman hurled his order to her and, not prepared to stay and see it in all probability disobeyed, strode to the sitting-room door, flung it open and flung it shut behind him.

B

Joyce heard him go up the stairs two at a time and heard his dressing-room door closed with the same violence. Very slowly she tilted up her glass and allowed the last drops of her cocktail to linger on her lips; then she rose, put her glass down and walking to the front door opened it, leaving it ajar and, leaning against the wall of Mr. Prentice's house, pressed the bell.

After a moment Markham opened the door in an unwilling fashion because in the Temple no one had called on Mr. Prentice in the evening unless they had been especially invited and, though he had heard the bell distinctly, he distrusted the evidence of his senses. When he saw Joyce's lips on the level of his eyes and his regard, travelling downward, became aware of her trousers and sandalled feet with their pink toe-nails, he began to distrust his senses again. Obviously the bell had been rung by mistake.

As his eyes slowly travelled up Joyce's figure to come to rest finally on her own, Markham made no attempt to ask her what she wanted; he just waited for an apology from her because she had come to the wrong door.

"I didn't expect to see you," Joyce said. "I thought yesterday you were a furniture remover. Not one of the men who actually moves the stuff, you know; but a foreman or a partner or something."

"You want to see Mr. Prentice?" Markham found his voice with difficulty. "You have an appointment?" he went on in tones of utter disbelief.

"Not exactly," Joyce replied. "As a matter of fact I just wanted to borrow some fish knives. We've got a party."

Markham prepared to shut the door.

"I'm afraid we don't lend cutlery," he said.

"I'm sure Mr. Prentice would if you asked him," Joyce replied with assurance.

At that moment the door of the sitting-room opened and Mr. Prentice came out of his study, his glasses perched on his forehead, and a diffident, enquiring look in his eyes. Joyce gave him a friendly smile.

"Could you lend me some fish knives?" she asked.

Mr. Prentice showed no sign of surprise at the request; in

truth, he had heard it, but it didn't appear to make any sense to him, his mind being wholly engrossed with the question of whether his client was responsible for the damage to his neighbour's ceiling by the stopping up of the balcony drain in his client's flat above.

"Fish knives?" he repeated as if he had never heard of such things.

"The handles are loose or off all mine," Joyce explained patiently.

Mr. Prentice, who could only see a half of her body through the half-closed door, turned impatiently to Markham.

"Please let this lady in," he said, "and shut the door or we'll have Lottie Spate all over the flower beds in a minute."

Markham hesitated a moment and then opened the door a little wider with great reluctance. Joyce gave him a dazzling smile as she wriggled through the small space.

"I don't want to come in really——" she began.

"Nonsense," Mr. Prentice interrupted her gently, recovering a little from his shyness. "Go and get this young lady some fish knives," he went on to Markham and, when the latter had gone, put his hand timidly on her arm to lead her towards the study. "I can't understand why Markham should keep a pretty woman hanging about on the doorstep," he continued. "Perhaps he doesn't approve of trousers." He pushed open the door and with a soft pressure on her arm urged her forward. "I've had occasion to study their wear lately and though I must say the disadvantages to some women are only too obvious they are not apparent on you."

In spite of his inconsequent chatter, delivered more to put himself at ease than her, Mr. Prentice noticed that for all her apparent self-possession Joyce went into the study without any eagerness. Indeed, he noticed that she hesitated perceptibly on the threshold and that her upright carriage grew even tauter, as if she was bracing herself up to perform a task which was distasteful to her; but once she was in the room she appeared to relax again and, as she surveyed the book-shelves, the table littered with papers and pieces of red and white tape, the armchair and the reading lamp, a ghost of a smile trembled a moment about her lips.

"I'm afraid this room is a little untidy," Mr. Prentice apologized, "but I am not in the habit of receiving beautiful women."

"Most people think I look like a prostitute," Joyce confessed.

Mr. Prentice took his glasses off and laid them down on the table near his books and papers.

"I think, my dear, you give most people, or they give themselves, credit for too much perspicacity." He gave his opinion very deliberately after considering her statement a moment. "In other days, of course, there would not have been anything odd about the assumption; but to-day I should hesitate to decide what a woman's profession was on the nod, so to speak. Death was said to be the great leveller; now it appears our forefathers were mistaken and it is democracy. It may well be in a hundred years' time that it won't matter at all which house you sleep in, or for that matter with whom you take your pleasure because all the houses and all the people will be standardized. So will their brains, and the conversation in one house will probably be the same as the conversation in another— education being served up in half-hour doses by broad-casting and television, and everyone adopting the viewpoint of the speakers."

"I'm not much interested in the future," Joyce admitted.

"You are in advance of your time," Mr. Prentice assured her. "I am only interested in the present myself; a time made a great deal more palatable by your presence." He paused. "By the way, have you come a long way in search of fish knives and how many do you want?"

Joyce sat down in his armchair and, picking up one of the many papers lying on the table, began to read it.

"I've only come from next door," she replied. "And I want four. Can you spare them?" She waved the paper at him. "What is all this about? It looks legal."

Mr. Prentice went to the door and shouted down the passage.

"Markham! The case of fish knives and forks."

"It is already wrapped up and lying on the hall table," came the answer.

Mr. Prentice shut the door again and, standing by it, one hand on his round paunch and the other on the door handle, gazed at Joyce. He thought she looked very slight and appealing in his large armchair and that the room had taken on a new lease of life. He went to the corner cupboard, a lacquered piece of wood from which most of the lacquer had peeled away.

"Will you have a glass of sherry, my dear? I always have one at this time. I had no idea you were my next door neighbour, though I have heard your voice indistinctly once or twice," he went on. "I've also seen a young man in the courtyard."

"My husband," Joyce admitted without any signs of enthusiasm. "My profession is that of married woman. At least that's what I sign in the space called occupation."

Mr. Prentice took the decanter and two glasses from the cupboard and, holding the latter one after the other against the light, made certain that there was no dust on them.

"I prefer that to spinster," he said affably. "There's something very melancholy about that word. Although, as a matter of fact, Paula is a spinster, and I don't find anything particularly sad about her."

"Don't you?" Joyce asked a little enigmatically. "I'd no idea you had met her." She began to read the paper again. "You're a barrister, I suppose?"

Mr. Prentice poured out the sherry and put a glass for her on the table beside her.

"I hope you've arrived at your conclusion from the papers on my table," he said, "and not from my deportment."

"Do you deal in the divorce court?" Joyce asked, putting the paper down and sipping her sherry.

"I practise on the Chancery side," Mr. Prentice answered. "I spend my time routing about in other people's wills, trampling over other people's land and unsettling other people's settlements." He sipped his sherry. "It seems very fashionable nowadays for married women to be interested in the divorce courts," he went on. "That's because the whole basis of marriage is wrong."

"What's wrong with it?" Joyce asked.

"Marriage, as I see it, is primarily a civil contract," Mr. Prentice explained, "and people who want to get married should be married by the state in the first place. That assures them and everyone else that having incurred legal obligations they will be made to carry them out in so far as the law of the land can compel them."

"I thought marriage was a sacrament."

"But vows are not taken to be broken," Mr. Prentice went on a little severely. "Civil contracts are continually being made and broken, and provided the one who breaks the contract pays the damages, no particular odium attaches to him. So it would be with a civil contract of marriage—indeed, if you've been already divorced that is your only safeguard now because the Church doesn't recognize remarriage whether you're the innocent or the guilty party."

"You want to do away with the sacrament altogether?"

"Certainly not, my dear," Mr. Prentice replied, a shocked expression spreading over his beatific face, "but I don't think people should play fast and loose with it. When a man comes of age he is given the latchkey of the house because he is presumed to have reached the years of discretion and is judged to be able to use the rooms properly. So at some point in married life the Bishops should hold up the key of the Church to the husband and wife and, if they take it in their hands and, opening the stiff lock, advance down the lonely aisle to the beflowered altar, then their steps should be irrevocable. In that way the Church would deserve the respect which is its due, and men and women would be saved from losing theirs."

"I wonder how many would do it?" Joyce asked more of herself than of Mr. Prentice.

"I don't think that really matters, does it?" he answered. "If no one did, then the Church would be dead; but if only one couple did so, its existence would be justified."

At that moment the bell rang with a long insistent whirr and, at the same time, the thud of a fist, though muffled by obstructions, was distinctly audible in the study. Mr. Prentice hastily put down his glass and turned his brown eyes, clouded with apprehension, towards the passage. Joyce hastily finished what sherry still remained and rising rapidly went towards the door with a muttered word of thanks, but before she could turn the handle it was flung violently open and her husband, with Markham hovering behind him, burst into the room.

"Do you know what the time is?" he shouted at his wife. Joyce looked at him coldly.

"Too late for high tea and too early for supper," she answered. "My husband, Mr. Prentice." She introduced them, but Norman paid no attention to his host.

"I've been trying to entertain the Bellamys for a quarter of an hour. There's no dinner and no you," Norman went on at the top of his voice.

"I'm afraid it is possibly my fault," Mr. Prentice put in suavely. "Or rather, my man Markham's. He has a habit of putting things away and forgetting where he put them. We had trouble in locating the fish knives."

"Damn the fish knives!" Norman exclaimed.

"I shan't dress for dinner," Joyce said. "That'll make everything quite all right." With which she went out and Markham, handing her the parcel, held the front door open.

"You might remind my husband we have people dining with us to-night," Joyce said to him and Markham watched her disappear into the next door house clasping the parcel to her chest.

Mr. Prentice regarded the angry young man diffidently; he was very afraid of violence and the strained, pale and drawn features of his companion caused him acute uneasiness.

"Er—have a glass of sherry, won't you?" he asked hastily.

He was looking at Norman, but actually he did not see him. What he saw was an old, comic picture book in which a little black boy, pursued by a tiger, attempted to allay the latter's progress and appetite by discarding his food and his clothes bit by bit. Mr. Prentice saw himself as the little black boy and Norman as the tiger.

"Sherry," Norman repeated vaguely.

"Your wife gave me the pleasure of——"

"Oh, she did, did she?" Norman interrupted him, his senses returning to a full appreciation of time and place.

"Then I will, if I may; and she can find out what it's like to be at the other end of the stick."

Mr. Prentice went hastily to the corner cupboard and took down another glass.

"I'm afraid I've been very rude to you," Norman went on. "I——" then he stopped abruptly and stared about him with an intensity that Mr. Prentice found a little disconcerting. "Good heavens!" he exclaimed, "you have altered this room around. I shouldn't have known it."

Mr. Prentice, who was pouring out the sherry into the glass, checked his hand and then continued to fill the glass.

"You knew this room well before?" he asked.

"I? Oh no, not well," Norman replied hastily. "Hardly at all, in fact." He moved forward and took his glass from Mr. Prentice. "Here's your very good health!" He sipped his sherry and, looking at the mass of papers on the table, raised his eyebrows. "I'm afraid my wife has disturbed you rather badly," he finished.

"I don't mind how often I am disturbed by a pretty woman," Mr. Prentice confessed.

Norman stared at him for a moment and, when he could find no trace of irony on Mr. Prentice's chubby face, laughed a little perfunctorily.

"I should have thought it all rather depended on the woman," he said.

"My dear young man," Mr. Prentice began dryly, "I am not disturbed by so many pretty women that I can afford to throw any of them into the discard. You, no doubt, have had plenty of opportunity to study the whole question and can afford to adopt an Olympian attitude in the matter. But for me who, whatever inclinations I may have, have had neither the opportunity nor the means to play Lothario, there is no question of selection."

"You appear to have had more than your fair share of good fortune," Norman answered dryly.

Mr. Prentice swept his hand slowly across the ever increasing baldness on his head and watched Norman out of the corner of his eyes, noticing that he was still, inch by inch, parcelling out the area of the room with quick glances.

"Cynicism in the young," remarked Mr. Prentice at length, "is not a thing to be deplored. After all, it is a symptom of change and I am not one of those who believe that all changes are for the worse; though, doubtless, when I am a really old man I shall arrive at that point of view. If the young are cynical it shows that they are dissatisfied and, if they aren't satisfied, then changes must be made. However, I doubt whether man and woman alter very much at heart. Superficial changes, yes—like your wife's trousers—but I don't find them symptomatic of a desire to bestride the world like a Colossus, and still be decently dressed."

Norman stretched out his hand and apparently in a state of amnesia refilled his glass from the decanter on the table.

"Man's not born a cynic," he replied. "The iron enters into his soul because he gets such a raw deal from women."

Mr. Prentice regarded him sympathetically.

"You have suffered much?" he hazarded.

He saw Norman's eyes suddenly clear as those of a man returning to consciousness and he recognized an alertness, clothed in a thin covering of suspicion.

"I!" Norman exclaimed. "I am not speaking of my particular experiences. I was making a general statement."

Mr. Prentice hastily averted his attention and seemed to concentrate all his energies on discovering whether there was not the smallest bit of cork in his glass.

"Did you, by any chance, know the former occupier of this house?" he asked. "But, of course, you must have," he added suavely.

"I don't know about must," Norman answered as if he did not wish to answer the question at all. "Did you ask Joyce?" he went on, and Mr. Prentice thought that the atmosphere in the room had unaccountably increased in density. It seemed to him that the question was not a casual one, but that the young man was eager to know the answer.

"I didn't," he replied.

"Ah!"

Mr. Prentice could not quite determine whether the exclamation was out of relief or surprise; but as nothing more came from his young guest's lips, and he saw the former negative expression settle on his features, he prodded his mind to life again.

"You were quite right to correct me," he said graciously, "and there is no must about it. One of the reasons, indeed the chief reason, why I live in a big city is that I am not bound to know the neighbours. In the country it is quite a different matter. News travels by the shop vans more regularly than the country post, and scandal has half a dozen wings wedded to its body. In a city, especially one the size of London, one lives in a sealed box if one chooses to do so, and if one doesn't other people have a way of sealing one's box for one."

Once again Mr. Prentice was aware that, when he had started talking, Norman was not really listening, but when he had finished his whole expression had changed so that he was again alert. It seemed to Mr. Prentice as if he was weighing every word he uttered and, turning them over in his mind, was trying to discover whether there was some hidden meaning, some allusion which was escaping him.

"As a matter of fact," he answered, "Joyce and I did know her slightly—much in the same way as we have got to know you." The tenseness of his muscles relaxed and once more a flaccid expression rolled down his face like a blind. "I forget now exactly how it came about—probably a shortage of fish knives again." He smiled a little nervously. "But you needn't worry about us as neighbours. I hold your views."

"My dear young man," Mr. Prentice broke it at once, "you must not think that I was referring to your wife or you," he added hastily, "when I talked about one's duty towards one's neighbour. I hope you will both come in and have a glass of sherry——"

"That's very kind of you," Norman interrupted perfunctorily. "But, as a matter of fact, Joyce and I are thinking of going away for a little. We aren't so lucky as to have a manservant or any other kind—and the work gets Joyce down a bit at times. Makes her nervy, you know," he finished a little lamely.

Mr. Prentice was on the point of airing his views on the mistaken theory to him that women suffered more from nervous diseases than men when Markham, who had put his ear to the panel of the door several times in the hope that the conversation was upon the point of ending, at length opened the door with resolution.

"Dinner is ready," he said.

The effect of the announcement was somewhat spoilt by the inrush of Lottie Spate who approached Mr. Prentice in an ecstasy of excitement and affection and, as her master fondled her, Norman gulped down the rest of his sherry.

"I'm sorry," he said, "it's time I went back."

Mr. Prentice walked with him to the door and, Lottie Spate having escaped into the paved courtyard, went out himself to retrieve the dog. He watched Norman enter Number 4 and, as he passed their open window on his way back to his own house with Lottie Spate at his heels, heard Joyce's voice, languid on the still air.

"You've missed the soup," she said, "and isn't it provoking, they aren't Catholics."

Mr. Prentice, closing his front door on himself and his dog, could make nothing of Joyce's allusion, but as he sat down to his own dinner his mind was full of other things.

"I thought we weren't going to be bothered by our neighbours," Markham said reproachfully as he handed him a dish of macaroni *au gratin*. "You remember I told you differently."

"I also remember that you said we shouldn't like them," Mr. Prentice observed.

"And I don't," Markham said.

Mr. Prentice helped himself to the macaroni and regarded the melancholy Markham with a pensive, but not altogether unfriendly, look.

"You apparently have that quality, not rare in women, but unusual in men," he said, "of being able to make up your mind at once whether you like a person or not. For my part I am always rather prejudiced in favour of pretty women; I admit that readily. As a matter of fact I'm rather proud of it; much in the same way as people like to advertise that they suffer from lumbago or liver or headaches. All the same," he went on, "that does not mean to say that my senses are atrophied or that I am like clay in their pretty hands."

"I had hoped," Markham said, "that we should continue as we began. Except for the curtains of Number 5 which were being constantly pulled apart and pulled to again, no one appeared to take any notice of our arrival."

"Well, they apparently did," Mr. Prentice replied dryly. "You haven't seen a little girl called Paula I suppose?" he asked.

"I haven't," Markham said with a certain satisfaction.

Mr. Prentice leaned back in his chair, and resting his elbows on its arms, put his fingers to make a bridge.

"It's rather curious about that couple next door," he said at length. "Did you notice anything odd?"

"The lady, if she was one, was very peculiar," Markham replied, and his distaste was very marked.

"I wasn't referring to her appearance," Mr. Prentice answered a little tartly. "I am sure if you had your way with women they'd all have long hair done up in buns, white blouses and long black skirts. I myself prefer a little provocation in the matter of dress. No," he went on as he placidly finished his macaroni, "the odd thing about her and also about her husband was that, though they were both a little curious about this house, they were both also constrained in it: especially the husband who seemed to be searching both the room and his mind. What do you think he was looking for?"

No answer came from Markham who, having snatched his plate away with surprising swiftness, had left the room to fetch the next dish. Mr. Prentice had been so absorbed in his own thoughts that he had not noticed his departure, but when he did not reply he observed his absence and transferred the question to Lottie Spate.

"What, Miss Spate?" he repeated. "Or who? You're a woman, Lottie, tell me why did the lady hesitate so long on the threshold of my study and then square her shoulders? She, who was so delightfully self-possessed; and why did her husband ask me whether I had asked his wife if she had known the late tenant? You think I am displaying bad taste in my curiosity? I am no quidnunc. I'm not a curious man. Yet I can't help wondering what——" he stopped abruptly as Markham returned with the next course and he helped himself mechanically.

"The brain's an odd box of tricks," he went on to Markham after a minute. "Why should I worry about these things? 'You can't live here, it belongs to Iris'. That's what the child said to me." He looked up. "By the way, Markham, do you know anyone's surname in this court?"

"I don't," Markham answered and the tone of his denial implied that he didn't want to know.

"Because I find myself thinking of Iris, Paula, Joyce and Norman," Mr. Prentice said. "I hope I haven't caught that distressing germ of vulgarity broadcast so regularly by the British Corporation. What shops do you deal with, Markham?"

The suddenness of the question found Markham without a ready answer and Mr. Prentice, to forestall the resentment that he saw rising on his manservant's face, continued hurriedly. "I only wondered," he said airily, as if it was of no importance to him, "whether you had gleaned the full name of the last tenant."

"I am not going to alter my shopping area because you change our house," Markham said. "I don't know why you wanted to come here; what with cars leaving at all times of night and the rows next door——"

"Rows, Markham?"

"You can't hear. My room's next door to their bedroom. You call this a quiet place!" He cast his eyes up to the ceiling as if to invoke the aid of celestial reinforcements. "The trouble with you is you get so wrapped up in your own thoughts," he finished, "you don't hear the half of what goes on around you."

Mr. Prentice put down his spoon and fork with great deliberation.

"Why haven't you told me about this before?" he asked.

"Because it's no business of mine—and in any case I only want a quiet night's rest."

"What else have you heard?" Mr. Prentice asked him, paying no attention to his outburst.

"What else?" Markham repeated. "Well, there's a child that cries pretty regularly—that's from Number 1."

"Ah, that will be Paula!" Mr. Prentice interrupted.

Markham gave no sign that he had heard the interruption.

"Whoever lives in Number 3 measured his length in his flower bed about one o'clock in the morning last night," he went on imperturbably.

"Are you implying——" Mr. Prentice began.

"I'm implying nothing," Markham went on sadly, "only people don't fall over flower beds on moonlight nights because it's dark."

"No," Mr. Prentice admitted. "And Number 2 and Number 5?"

"I haven't heard a squeak out of them whoever they are, but that doesn't mean they don't squeak," he finished hastily.

Mr. Prentice went on eating his pudding and considered the set of circumstances as a whole.

"Well, it's no business of ours," he said, at length, without much conviction.

"That's what I was telling you," Markham replied, "but all the same things could be quieter—much. There was none of this sort of thing in the Temple, though I don't say I haven't seen a barrister or two the worse for wear sometimes."

Mr. Prentice rose sharply from his chair and, followed by Lottie Spate, went into his study where he picked up the brief upon which he had been engaged when he had been interrupted, and awaited his coffee. He was followed by Lottie Spate who curled herself at his feet and regarded the empty grate with jaundiced eyes.

It was very much later when Mr. Prentice gathered the papers together and, having glanced at his fee which he thought inadequate, clearly marked on the brief, tied the pink tape around them. He should have finished a full hour previously, but the interruptions had claimed their penalty and he saw with a little surprise that it was after midnight.

Knocking his pipe out against the cold grate, he awakened the dog who, discovering that the moment had arrived when the final walk would be taken, rose to her feet, stretched herself and regarded first Mr. Prentice and then the door with intelligent anticipation.

It was a lovely night and Mr. Prentice, standing in the courtyard, looked upwards through the motionless, feathery leaves of the ash tree to the heavens, lightened by an argent moon. Faintly in the nearby highway he could hear the intermittent rumble of the occasional traffic and here and there, in the small space of the vast heavens which he could see, a star fought bravely for recognition.

"What is beauty?" Mr. Prentice murmured to himself. "That's the sort of question people keep on asking and everyone says it lies in the eyes of the beholder and that, therefore, it is impossible to define." He moved forward slowly to lead Lottie Spate out of the courtyard. "But everyone would consider this evening's sky beautiful. Therefore that is beauty. But why——" He had lowered his head to watch where he was going and something glittered at his feet on the uneven flagstones. Leaving his question in the air he bent down to pick up the object and turned it round and round in his stubby fingers. It was a plain circlet of gold.

Mr. Prentice looked about him, but except for a faint chink of light on the first floor of Number 1 there was no sign that anyone was awake. Seeing Lottie Spate advancing with purpose towards the flower bed under that house, Mr. Prentice hastened to head her off and, transferring the ring to his waistcoat pocket, led the dog through the archway to the street, standing in which was a very expensive motor car about which there was something vaguely familiar. Then he remembered that when first he had come to look at the house he had had difficulty in getting into the courtyard at all because of a long, sleek black car. This was the same one, Mr. Prentice had no doubt of it and, as he fingered the ring in his pocket to make sure it was still there, he caught himself wondering to whom the car belonged, and he thought of the light on the first floor of Number 1.

Lottie Spate had ceased to range and, coming back to

him, waited for him to lead her back to Number 6; but Mr. Prentice appeared to be in no hurry as he stood in the centre of the gateway of the courtyard and looked at the dim parking lights of the car, while the tranquillity of the night tossed his soul in its cotton wool.

"And another thing that is beautiful to everyone," he murmured to himself, "is a calm warm sea with the moon tripping lightly on the ripples. At what point then, do people begin to disagree?"

He thought about that for a moment and had just made up his mind that he would be fortunate if he arrived at a positive answer by the time he died when he heard some unsteady footsteps, and a man whose approach had been masked by the car, skirted it with some difficulty.

Mr. Prentice turned away precipitately and dived beneath the archway only to find that far from avoiding the stranger, the man was in the courtyard with him. Not only that, but he was actually speaking to him.

"Do you live here?" the stranger asked.

Mr. Prentice hesitated.

"Because if you don't," the stranger went on, "I'm in favour of you clearing out and taking your dog with you. This place is becoming too crowded altogether."

"I do live here," Mr. Prentice said.

The stranger, wiping his hand a little uncertainly across his mouth and swaying very slightly, looked at him suspiciously.

"What number?" he asked.

"Number 6, as a matter of fact," Mr. Prentice replied with just that touch of dignity which he hoped would close the conversation in his favour. The stranger looked at him more closely.

"I prefer Iris," he said. "Definitely. Nevertheless——" he stopped abruptly, the pronunciation not being to his liking, and began again. "Nevertheless," he went on, "it behoves one to be hospitable to one's neighbours. Come in and have a drink." He went towards Number 3 without waiting for an answer and, a sudden shaft of light hitting the court-yard at Mr. Prentice's feet, Mr. Prentice made haste to escape it. It came, he noticed, from the first floor room of Number 1 where he dimly saw the head and shoulders of a woman; but as quickly as the curtains had been drawn back, they were pulled together again and Mr. Prentice, feeling acutely uncomfortable, was about to run across to his own door when the stranger called to him in what seemed to Mr. Prentice to be a voice of thunder, even if the roll was uncertain.

"Come on, don't hang about," the stranger said and Mr. Prentice, after casting anxious eyes at the blank windows of the other houses and wondering whether Markham had awakened, hastily came over to the door of Number 3 where the stranger had at length found the proper place in which to put his key. A light flooded the hall and Mr. Prentice shut the door behind himself and his dog.

Mr. Prentice noticed at once that Number 3 was designed architecturally in precisely the same manner as his own house, but there the similarity ended for the occupant, who had with some little difficulty found the light switch in the sitting-room, had very different ideas on furniture and furnishings from Mr. Prentice.

The upright chairs were constructed of what, to Mr. Prentice, looked like tubular steel, flowers made from glass stood stiffly in bizarre vases and armchairs of bright, brown leather looked clean but uninviting. Mirrors with bevelled edges and no frames were screwed into the walls and pictures of startling colours and of baffling subjects flanked them.

Mr. Prentice stood and blinked while the owner opened a shiny veneered cabinet that seemed to Mr. Prentice to contain more bottles of different shapes and sizes than he ever remembered seeing. Before it the owner hovered like some alchemist, swaying slightly and peering at the labels as if he had myopia.

"What's it to be?" he asked.

Mr. Prentice made a gesture of refusal.

"Really," he began, "I don't think that——"

"If you can't make up your own mind, I'll make it up for you," he interrupted Mr. Prentice and, seizing a bottle, poured out a generous tot of what Mr. Prentice hoped would prove to be whisky and not brandy or yellow chartreuse.

"You can squirt the soda in yourself," he went on when he had made a very small splash in his own.

Mr. Prentice went diffidently toward the cabinet.

"This is very nice of you," he said pleasantly, though he didn't feel very pleasant. He wanted to go to bed and he could see by the mournful expression in Lottie Spate's eyes that she also had no zest for further adventure. "By the way, I'm afraid I don't know your name," Mr. Prentice concluded as he drowned the whisky in as much soda as he could get into the glass.

"Speed's the name," answered his host, falling backwards into an armchair the moment the frame touched the back of his calves. "As a matter of fact, this isn't very nice of me at all. I'm by way of pleasing myself, not you."

Mr. Prentice, who had been vaguely aware that Mr. Speed was a very big man, suddenly realised how very big he was for, though the armchair was by no means a small one, he not only filled it with his wide shoulders and broad frame, but spilled himself out of it as well. A leonine head, freely flecked with grey hair, deep lines above the mouth that creased his cheeks and muddy green eyes made Mr. Speed an impressive, if not at first sight a particularly likeable figure of a man; but when he smiled, as he did suddenly for no particular reason, Mr. Prentice found him immediately softened and in an odd way unexpectedly charming.

"My name's Prentice," Mr. Prentice ventured at length when Mr. Speed continued to smile into the unlit electric fire, but otherwise showed no very obvious signs of life. Mr. Speed took a sip of his whisky and soda and made no effort to acknowledge his guest. "I was just taking my dog out for a final walk when——"

"I don't think I like dogs," Mr. Speed interrupted him, giving Lottie Spate a long and bitter stare. "In fact, I am sure I don't," he went on, "but I prefer them to horses. Do you know anything about horses?" He gave Mr. Prentice a long and unfocused glance and, just as Mr. Prentice was about to reply, continued himself. "No, I can see you don't." He paused and a flush of anger made his face redder than ever. "When you think of the amount of time and money that mankind spends on trying to make a horse do such an obvious thing as gallop consistently!" he exclaimed, flinging out his enormous hand and throwing his head back. "Well, I ask you!"

"I thought the main object of horse racing was to ensure that the horses shouldn't run consistently," Mr. Prentice observed and, thinking that he saw signs of his companion's anger overwhelming him, went on hastily. "I mean if they did you couldn't very well bet at all. Not that I'm a betting man," he finished hurriedly.

"Then I think you are somewhat foolish," Mr. Speed said flatly. "It is plainly better to make money without working if it is possible, and horse racing is one of the few ways of doing it. The world is a very unpleasant place to-day, and work is one of the most unpleasant things about it."

Mr. Prentice moved uneasily in his chair, but summoning up all his courage eventually replied.

"Surely you have a duty to the state. You should work partly for it and partly for yourself," he said diffidently, being a little afraid that if he aired his views more forcibly he might find himself broken in half and tossed through the window into the courtyard.

"The state has a duty to me," retorted Mr. Speed. "It was here before I was and, God help it, it will be here after me." He regarded Mr. Prentice sourly. "And what is democracy?" he asked truculently. "The rule of the wise by the stupid," he answered his own question in the same breath.

"You want a benevolent oligarchy, is that it?"

Mr. Speed looked at him, suspicion darkling his eyes.

"I'm not sure I know what that means," he replied running the words one into the other. "But the object of life is to take from it all the happiness that the short span allows you to get hold of."

"Obviously everyone can't be happy; one must, therefore, strive for the greatest good of the greatest number," Mr. Prentice objected mildly.

"That only means that everyone is miserable," Mr. Speed said. "And by God, they are!" he added forcibly. "In the old days at any rate someone had something; now no one has anything—except people like me, and we spend our time and money trying to find oblivion." He looked at his nearly empty glass. "And nearly succeeding sometimes. The best moments in life are those when you're drunk or asleep; and the only fun one gets out of consciousness is the fun of seeing other men, like you, do all the work." He walked unsteadily towards the cabinet and Mr. Prentice leaned back as his enormous bulk passed erratically in front of him. "As a matter of fact," Mr. Speed continued, "the idea has been found pleasing by more and more people. Indeed, it is sometimes quite difficult to find anyone who's doing any honest work at all in these days. Idling used to be a woman's job; but they threw away the substance of happiness for the shadow, and men were pretty quick in letting them do it." He half filled his glass with whisky again and gave it a squirt of soda.

"Women," echoed Mr. Prentice softly, who wasn't very certain exactly what Mr. Speed meant, but saw an opportunity to turn his host's conversation into less abstract channels. "Talking of women," he went on in a rather bolder voice, "what was Iris like?"

"Iris," Mr. Speed repeated vaguely, working his unsteady passage to the chair.

"You said you preferred her to me—definitely," Mr. Prentice prompted him.

Mr. Speed swayed in front of Mr. Prentice for a moment but Mr. Prentice noticed that his eyes, which a second since had seemed as vague and uncertain as his speech, cleared rapidly, and something akin to suspicion awoke in them.

"I was talking—or thought I was—about upper class women in general, if the epithet means anything to-day," he said.

Mr. Prentice made a hasty movement of apology.

"I'm afraid I've been guilty of vulgar curiosity," he began. "It is really of no importance," he went on hurriedly. "It was the little girl that really started it," he finished.

"Which little girl?" Mr. Speed asked.

"Her name's Paula and she lives in Number 1," Mr. Prentice replied.

"And she cries," Mr. Speed added. "No children and no dogs should be allowed."

"If no children were allowed, there'd be——"

"No grown-up people; none at all," Mr. Speed broke in. "And a damned good thing too! This isn't a world any more. In the old days, at any rate, some of the people were happy some of the time; now no one's happy any of the time unless he's unconscious: and that's an expensive panacea," he repeated himself as he eyed his whisky. "Do you know why she cries?" he asked.

Mr. Prentice admitted that he didn't.

"She cries because Iris has gone away and her own mother hasn't," he said.

"Is her mother the lady who looked out of the window when we came in?" Mr. Prentice asked.

Mr. Speed suddenly decided to sit down and resumed his seat, staring into the unlit electric stove once more. Mr. Prentice thought there was something forlorn about him, like an old ship waiting to be broken up. Suddenly he appeared to have lost the thread of the conversation altogether and to be unaware of the presence of his guest.

"It's an odd thing," Mr. Speed muttered at length, and Mr. Prentice believed he did not realize that he was speaking aloud, "it's an odd thing," he repeated, "that what one can have for the taking one doesn't take: and what one can't have one breaks one's neck trying to get." He took another sip of his whisky and gazed moodily in front of him; at least that was what Mr. Prentice thought he was doing until suddenly the glass slipped from his fingers to the carpet.

Both Mr. Prentice and Lottie Spate sat up and both watched Mr. Speed expectantly, but when he made no movement, Mr. Prentice approached him carefully to find that he had sunk into that state which he regarded as blessed. Mr. Prentice hesitated, wondering what he should do. Then he carefully put his own glass in the cabinet, went quietly toward the door with Lottie Spate at his heels, turned off the lights in the hall, opened the front door and shut it gently behind him and his dog.

Out in the courtyard the moon still turned the night to silver except for a golden thread that came from behind the curtains of Number 1. Mr. Prentice tiptoed into his own house and was just shutting the door behind him with a sigh of relief when the hallway was flooded with light and, looking up, he saw Markham looking down at him, his lean, cadaverous form appearing a little grotesque wrapped in its old frayed dressing-gown.

The sight filled Mr. Prentice not only with amazement, but with a curious feeling of unreality. He had never before seen Markham without his hair brushed and, now that he came to think of it, he couldn't ever remember his spare figure clad in anything but the conventional clothes of a manservant. He regarded him with open-mouthed surprise and even Lottie Spate began to make the snuffling noises in which she generally engaged before she let out a bark.

But it wasn't so much the way that Markham was dressed that upset Mr. Prentice; he soon recovered from the initial surprise of that. It was the expression on his face which began to flood Mr. Prentice with a feeling of vague disquiet. There was more than a glimpse of apprehension in his eyes but, as Mr. Prentice peered up the stairs, he watched the uneasiness disappear and saw relief take its place. The whole episode was momentary, but in that moment Mr. Prentice had felt worried.

"I didn't know where you'd gone," Markham said at length in answer to the unspoken question in Mr. Prentice's eyes. Mr. Prentice thought the remark somewhat odd. "You didn't say you were going out," Markham added as if he thought a further explanation was necessary.

"I only took Lottie Spate for her usual walk," Mr. Prentice answered mildly.

"You were so long away I thought something must have happened to you," Markham said a little defiantly.

"Why?"

Markham considered the question a moment. It seemed to Mr. Prentice that he was searching desperately for a reasonable answer and searching in vain. At length, he shrugged his shoulders.

"I don't know," he replied at last. "Are you coming up to bed now?"

Mr. Prentice nodded, and Markham turned away from the landing at the top of the stairs and, entering his own room, closed the door behind him. Lottie Spate scrambled into her basket, curled herself up and, emitting a sigh as evidence that she alone bore all the sorrows of the world upon her back, closed her eyes.

Mr. Prentice regarded her thoughtfully for a second, then slowly mounting the stairs, went into his own room, snapping out the staircase light to leave the hall in darkness. As he took off his coat he looked thoughtfully about him as if to make sure that nothing was out of place and, indeed, nothing was. There stood his high single bed—he had no use for the modern divan that laid one's head into the dust; his walnut dressing-table with its mirror, the easy chair and the hard one and his fitted cupboards. It was a somewhat spartan room, but it was very clean.

As he pulled off his waistcoat his finger and thumb felt something hard in its pocket, and he remembered the wedding ring. He took it out and, walking across to the bed light, examined it curiously. At first sight it seemed to be the fellow of any other plain gold band, but as he looked at it more closely he saw that some letters had been engraved on the inside. He had no great difficulty in reading them. "For Joyce on her wedding day" was what he read, and he put the gold circle down on his bedside table with great care before he resumed his disrobing.

Rings, he told himself, and especially wedding rings, did not end up on flagged stones by chance. Wedding rings, indeed, had a way of staying on the finger through all vicissitudes; until death sometimes. This was no careless mislaying and its import was obvious. Mr. Prentice sighed and immediately began to wonder what he should do. He could not, he felt, go hat in hand to his next door neighbour and, begging her pardon, calmly hand back her ring, explaining that he had found it in the courtyard. Perhaps she hadn't wanted it to be found, or perhaps she had wanted it to be found and returned by someone else—her husband, for instance.

"If only one could get rid of one's responsibilities by just throwing them out of the window," Mr. Prentice muttered to himself, going to his window and opening it for the night. As he did so, he heard the noise of a car being started and saw the headlights throw a golden stream of light across the gateway. There was a sudden dull whirr as the engine became alive and the car shot away towards the main street. Mr. Prentice's eyes, like the wheeling ray of a lighthouse, swept the windows of the three houses opposite. Number 1 was now in darkness; there was a faint light in the sitting-room of Number 3 where, doubtless, Mr. Speed was still in his beatific state and Number 5 remained apparently without life as it had done all the evening. Mr. Prentice pulled his curtains together and added one more odd piece of knowledge about his neighbours to his scanty store. In spite of Mr. Speed's deplorable condition Mr. Prentice was sure that Mr. Speed was not an habitual drunkard, and that he was a new convert to the faith that the best way to lose sight of the ugly face of the world was to spirit oneself away.

The next morning Mr. Prentice put the wedding ring into a nice clean envelope and, as he made his way to his chambers, thrust it through the letter box of Number 4. He had hoped that his action was unobserved, but just as he was withdrawing his hand, he heard a patter of feet and Paula came from behind the trunk of the large ash tree from where she had watched him.

"Are you a postman?" she asked. "Have you any letters for Number 1?"

Mr. Prentice hastily backed away from Number 4 and, with his brief-case in his hand, denied the charge.

"Then what's in there?" Paula asked, pointing to the brief-case. "And what were you putting in the letter box?"

Mr. Prentice found it very difficult to follow his own maxim which required that children should be told the truth.

"It's a case for carrying my papers," he said, ignoring the second part of the question altogether. "What are you doing out here at this time in the morning and why haven't you been to see me?" he went on very quickly, hoping the child would not pursue the matter any further.

Paula put her fingers to her lips and, after casting an

anxious glance towards the windows on the first floor of Number 1, whispered:

"Sh—mother's asleep." She looked up at Mr. Prentice. "She told me I wasn't to come and see you."

"Did she?" Mr. Prentice asked.

Paula nodded solemnly.

"Yes," she said. "Mother doesn't like me to talk to strangers."

"But you and I are not strangers," Mr. Prentice said.

"Mother doesn't like me to talk to anyone here," Paula replied.

"What about Iris?" Mr. Prentice asked.

Paula looked at him and her eyes opened a little wider.

"She hasn't come back, has she?" she asked anxiously. "She——"

"Paula!" A voice echoed across the courtyard. "Come here at once."

Paula turned and as she ran towards Number 1 she began to cry. Mr. Prentice turned and was about to intercede for her, but before he could get the words out of his mouth, the door of Number 1, which had been half opened, was shut with a certain amount of vehemence. He had a glimpse of a young woman with untidy fair hair and a gay peignoir; and he had a feeling as he went towards the gateway that his progress, which he tried to make without embarrassment, was being remarked. Yet such was his shyness that he dared not look back until he was outside the courtyard; then out of the corner of his eye he cast back one fleeting glance and saw at the far end of the flagged stones what he thought to be a fine figure of a man—a man whom he had never seen before but whom he judged must be the occupant of Number 5. He was looking at Number 1 and his face was eloquent with disgust.

Mr. Prentice's days at the Law Courts were never marked by anything which could be called unusual or even unexpected. He dodged from one Chancery court to another, in the more important cases supporting a silk and, in the smaller ones, shuffling to his feet with a mumbled "May it please your lordship." He was rarely briefed in any very big action and had only once in his career found himself in the House of Lords. However, by picking up a few guineas here and a few guineas there he managed to make a fairly comfortable living.

Yet there was no denying, and he did not deny it to himself, that there were days, and it seemed to him that these were becoming more frequent, when he found life dull and monotonous and wished he had more of the spice of variety that came the way of his colleagues on the Common Law side. He also appeared to have more leisure of late; that was not owing to any falling off in his practice, but was due to the fact that, while it had remained fairly stationary, his own experience had not, and he now cut the unessentials away in a much shorter time to leave the bare bones.

In spite of his apparently good-humoured face and his generous paunch Mr. Prentice was worried. He had moved into St. Anne's Court a couple of days ago, and the premium that he had had to pay to the Earl's solicitors for his sixteen year lease and the charges for removal and redecoration had made a very severe hole in his savings. He had left himself with barely sufficient to make ends meet, and he had made a breach in his sea wall that would be very dangerous if the tides of ill-health or paucity of work began to beat against it.

Still, there things were and nothing could be done about them he told himself philosophically as he sipped the cup of tea and ate the couple of biscuits which his clerk had brought him in the moment the courts had risen for the day and he was once more back in his chambers. Furthermore, there was nothing wrong with the clerk; he worked well for the whole chambers, and Mr. Prentice knew that the fault lay in himself and not with anyone else that he had got so far and no further on the legal ladder.

He could always reduce his expenses by getting rid of Markham, but he obviously had to have someone and he very much doubted whether Markham would go. That train of thought brought him to Markham's behaviour on the previous night. He was, as Mr. Prentice well knew, the most imperturbable of men; he might look lugubrious, he might argue, he might be rude or ungracious, but at no time was he taken out of his stride and whatever he might be feeling little or nothing of his emotions, except melancholy, was visible. Yet Markham had looked not exactly frightened, but certainly apprehensive, and his condition was not due to the fact that he had heard a noise downstairs and had been afraid that burglars were abroad; nor could it be due, he felt, to any fracas which the young couple next door may have started. No, it wasn't either of those things, Mr. Prentice felt sure, because Markham must have known he was out since there were no lights downstairs and his bedroom door was wide open; and if the raised voices next door had disturbed him, he would certainly have said so, but he had not mentioned it then nor when he had called him in the morning, nor later when he had handed him his breakfast. But Mr. Prentice, who had studied his manservant surreptitiously over the newspaper, thought he had looked finer-drawn than usual as if he had slept badly and without comfort.

Mr. Prentice did not think that he was particularly susceptible to atmosphere, though there had been times in his life when the powerful emotions felt by his fellow beings had so charged the air that he had himself experienced brief moments when his reason was subjugated to his heart. Such experiences had been nearly all brought about by some fear which overwhelmed his companions first and finally engulfed him, not because he himself was afraid, but because the rising wave of hysteria submerged him and his will-power cracked. Now, in retrospect, he felt again a touch of uneasiness.

When he had said that one of the chief reasons for living in London was that in a big town there was no necessity to know one's neighbours, and that the bigger the town the more private was one's existence, and privacy was one of the things he most coveted, he spoke the truth. He had no desire to peep behind the curtains of other people's lives, and up till the moment when he had walked into St. Anne's Court he had never wanted to do so; but he was conscious now that he was just as guilty as anyone who made a habit of watching behind curtained windows or listening behind closed doors.

Not that he himself had descended so far as that, or would; but the behaviour of his neighbours had impinged itself on his mind for the first time that he could remember. They had become important people to him who had breadth and height and depth and were no longer shadows that had no substance. And he couldn't understand why.

"It wasn't as if these people mean anything to me," he muttered to himself as he nibbled his biscuit. "In any case, I hardly know them and probably won't know any more of them unless I deliberately thrust myself upon them. But I cannot help wondering why Joyce was so reluctant to enter my study; why her husband parried so obviously my question about the late owner, and why Mr. Speed became so quickly alert when I mentioned her name, and why the late owner should have let the lease of her house go and why she told the little girl she was coming back if she wasn't. But it wasn't all that which really drew my attention to her. I had her in my mind before, although I didn't know it at the time. It was the marigolds." He paused and regarded his half empty cup of tea intently. "Yes, it was the marigolds," he decided, and he went on talking aloud to himself because, being a lonely man, he had taken to the habit and he had found, too, that by reading his briefs aloud the points became more sharply delineated in his mind. "She isn't cut to the ordinary pattern; she won't follow the crowd. No stocks for her. Because she doesn't like them? No, I don't think so. But she's not going to do the same as everyone else until she is convinced that everyone else is right and she is wrong. And if she is wrong, then what? Does she persist? Or does she give in gracefully? That's the test of character."

The thoughts of Mr. Prentice lost themselves in a labyrinth of speculation which left his original question deserted at the entrance of the maze, and when suddenly he realized that he could not find his way back again, he jumped to his feet and, gathering his briefs together for the next day, shattered the whole structure. With a gesture of annoyance at his own behaviour he shut the door of his chambers behind him, and with a nod to his clerk bade him good night. Out in the street he tried to keep his mind strictly to the problem of catching his bus, knowing that he had left his chambers unexpectedly early and that his clerk had not approved.

The afternoon sun was filtering through the ash tree when he came to the entrance of the Court and stood for a moment framed in the gateway, a hot and uncomfortable figure in his shabby homburg, black coat and striped trousers. The scene that lay before his eyes was peaceful enough and nothing stirred except a cabbage white butterfly that fluttered and settled, fluttered and settled among the stocks; this was the tranquillity that he had sought and, at that moment, captured. Even the rumble of the traffic in the high road was stilled, or appeared to be, and Mr. Prentice felt that at that minute eternity had kept an appointment with him. So long as the silence lasted he remained in the gateway, tubby, rosy-faced and hot, his black brief-case dangling slackly from his hand, a commonplace figure enough—an ordinary man trammelled in the infinite.

Then the door of Number 5 opened and immediately it seemed to Mr. Prentice that the roar of traffic in the high road had never sounded so loudly, and that it was indeed true that peace was indivisible.

Mr. Prentice, the moment the door of Number 5 opened, began automatically to walk in the direction of his own house and, as he walked, his footsteps sounded very loudly in his ear, and he became self-conscious under what he sensed, rather than knew, to be the scrutiny of the tall man whom he had seen standing in much the same place when he had set off for his chambers in the morning. The nearer he came to his own door, the more Mr. Prentice wished that he had not halted in the gateway and that he was already in his own study; but when he reached the doorway and his hand was in his pocket fumbling for his key, he suddenly took himself to task for behaving in such an absurd way and, just to convince himself that he had as much right in the court-yard as anyone else, he withdrew his hand and, stooping down over his marigolds, busied himself trying to find a few dead heads that he could pull away. A shadow fell across the bed and he straightened himself out to find the occupier of Number 5 gazing down at him.

"Good afternoon; my name's Fawcett. I've made one or two attempts already to welcome you," the tall man said.

Mr. Prentice found himself looking at a black tie on a very thin chest.

"That's very kind of you," he stammered, raising his eyes to see what kind of man was confronting him. He saw a narrow head with a grey shock of hair, an aquiline nose whose flesh was drawn tightly across the bone, a short upper lip, a thin uncompromising mouth and a pair of eyes that appeared to search the depths of his being. They were topped by a pair of thick black eyebrows, well threaded with grey hair.

"I'd have asked my wife to call," Mr. Fawcett went on, "only you appear to be a bachelor?" His voice had a slight questioning inflection as if to ask whether this was indeed the truth.

Mr. Prentice looked a little uncomfortable.

"Yes, I am," he admitted. "It's very kind of you. One expects those kind of courtesies in the country, but not in town—no, not in town."

"One has a duty to one's neighbour," Mr. Fawcett said.

Mr. Prentice, casting his eyes down again and noting a dead marigold, hastily stooped and removed the flower.

"Yes," he stammered uncertainly, "I suppose one has."

"There is no supposition about it," declared Mr. Fawcett. "It is a fact. Perhaps not always palatable, but a fact."

"Yes, of course," Mr. Prentice said hastily. Then an idea struck him and he became more at ease as he straightened himself out. "And have you called on all the inhabitants in the Court?" he asked.

"Once," Mr. Fawcett answered.

Mr. Prentice's smile beamed suddenly in his rosy face as he fumbled again in his pocket for his keys.

"Come in, won't you?" he asked him.

Mr. Fawcett didn't hesitate.

"Thank you, I will," he answered.

The uncompromising acceptance took Mr. Prentice momentarily aback and he missed the lock with the key at the first attempt. Eventually, however, he unlocked the door and, with a muttered apology, preceded his guest into the sitting-room, where he put his brief-case and his hat on a chair in the corner while Mr. Fawcett, tall and unbending, stood in the middle of the room, watching him.

Mr. Prentice, feeling uncomfortable again under the scrutiny, hastily pulled out his cigarette case and offered his guest a cigarette, but Mr. Fawcett waved it away with the utmost contempt.

"I don't smoke," he said.

"A whisky and soda, then, or perhaps a glass——" Mr. Prentice began.

"I don't drink," Mr. Fawcett broke in and Mr. Prentice, who had no very friendly feelings towards his guest before the denial, now regarded him with no enthusiasm at all; but he had asked him in for a definite purpose and he didn't lose sight of it. Far from showing any lack of good humour he sat down in his armchair and indicated the other one to Mr. Fawcett.

"I daresay you're perfectly right," he said, lighting his cigarette. "We should all be better without them. On the other hand I am a hedonist; though my pursuit of happiness is somewhat restricted by my pocket."

Mr. Fawcett sat down, an upright figure even in the armchair and his eyes raked Mr. Prentice from head to foot.

"A pernicious creed," he replied. "The pursuit of happiness is not the purpose of our life on this earth. We are here solely to try and render ourselves fit for the next life—that is the real goal; and it isn't to be reached except through right living."

Mr. Prentice listened to this outburst with a certain astonishment. Mr. Fawcett appeared to be delivering a sermon at him.

"And what happens to all those people who don't attain the required standard?" he asked.

"They cease to be," Mr. Fawcett answered with conviction. "There is no survival for them. One moment they are: and the next they are not." He snapped his fingers to illustrate their disappearance.

"You mean they do not survive—if only to expiate their sins?" Mr. Prentice said.

"Exactly," replied Mr. Fawcett. "It is as if they had never been born." He snapped his fingers again.

"I'm not so sure that isn't an improvement on hell," Mr. Prentice put in gently after he had given the matter a little thought; but Mr. Fawcett's reactions were far from gentle. He jumped from his seat and stood over Mr. Prentice, banging his closed fist into his open palm to emphasize his points.

"The world is spinning into the slime of dishonour, degradation and decay at an appalling rate," he shouted at him. "And no one cares. Soon everyone will have forgotten what the true standard of right living is because they keep on changing the yardstick." He appeared to be suddenly conscious of his own raised voice and belligerent attitude and, passing his hand across his eyes as if to wipe out the scene in his mind's eye, sank back into his chair, limp and trembling. "I told Iris as much," he muttered.

Mr. Prentice, who had felt very uncomfortable when confronted by such a fanatical exhibition, watched the fires damped down with considerable relief, and waited eagerly for his guest to continue, not upon his theory of the next world, or lack of it, but upon Iris. Mr. Fawcett, however, appeared to have sunk into a sort of coma, staring in front of him and muttering to himself.

"Iris?" Mr. Prentice repeated the name softly and slowly.

Mr. Fawcett gradually recovered his self-possession; his eyes cleared and his lips, becoming still, set once more in a thin uncompromising line. He pulled himself up in the chair by the arms and stared at Mr. Prentice from under his bushy eyebrows.

"Iris," Mr. Fawcett reiterated eagerly. "You know where she is? I can see you do; that's what I came to ask you. Please tell me at once."

To say that Mr. Prentice was taken aback is to use altogether too mild an expression. He sat facing his guest with his mouth hanging open and his eyes wide with astonishment; an astonishment which increased as Mr. Fawcett continued.

"I must know. You must tell me," he said, and the fires so lately doused rose again. "I must see her again, don't you understand? It's a matter of life and death to me. I can't sleep."

"But why should I know where she is?" Mr. Prentice asked when he had found his tongue. "As a matter of fact," he confided, "I was going to ask you the same question."

"You don't know?" Mr. Fawcett asked incredulously. "But you took the house from her. You must know. You must."

Mr. Prentice made a bridge with his hands and, rubbing his middle fingers up and down the sides of his nose, contemplated the agitated Mr. Fawcett with greater attention. It was gradually becoming apparent to him that the late occupant of his house had exercised a very special influence over the other inhabitants in the Court. What the nature of the influence was he hadn't the least idea; but first Paula, then the young married couple next door, then the elephantine and unsteady Mr. Speed and now the fanatical Mr. Fawcett, had all in one way or another served to prod Mr. Prentice's curiosity, and each one of them had aroused it further, not so much by what they had said, but by what they had left unsaid. As he turned the problem over and over in his mind and reviewed it much in the same way as he would a legal poser, Mr. Prentice suddenly became aware that Mr. Fawcett was no longer sitting in the armchair opposite to him, but was once more standing above him, his thin and flushed face thrust immediately above his own.

"You are lying," Mr. Fawcett shouted at him. "There's no such thing as truth to-day. Everyone has forgotten it."

Mr. Prentice, thoroughly alarmed for the moment, huddled himself deeper into his armchair.

"I assure you I am not lying," he stammered. "As a matter of fact I don't make a habit of telling lies. As I've already told someone else I took a direct lease from——"

"Told who?" Mr. Fawcett burst in.

"The little girl from Number 1," Mr. Prentice replied hastily.

Mr. Fawcett grinned; it was not a pleasant sight and Mr. Prentice was reminded, he could not think why, of a hyena.

c

"I should hardly call that fallen woman, Mrs. Dawson, a little girl!" Mr. Fawcett exclaimed.

"Fallen woman!" reiterated Mr. Prentice in some atonishment, more at the phrase than at its implication.

Mr. Fawcett was standing upright again, his lean, cadaverous body swaying slightly and his hands clasped behind his back so tightly that the knuckles were bloodless.

"I have written to the Earl's solicitors twice," he said. "I will not tolerate a disorderly house here—or anywhere else if I had my way—but under my nose, certainly not."

Mr. Prentice experienced, over and above his emotion of curiosity, a certain excitement, but all he uttered was a meaningless phrase.

"Really! You don't mean to say——" he exclaimed.

"Cars arrive and leave at all times of the night," went on Mr. Fawcett. "It's degrading; it's revolting."

"Are you quite sure——" began Mr. Prentice.

"Sure!" Mr. Fawcett exclaimed. "I don't need ocular proof to recognize the obvious." He grinned again. "Little girl, you call her." He thrust his head forward and his eyes bored into those of Mr. Prentice. "Have you been trafficking in forbidden love?" he asked.

"Good gracious, no," stammered Mr. Prentice, though he experienced a slightly pleasurable feeling at the thought that he should be taken for such an abandoned man. "I was talking of the girl, her daughter, I presume."

"Her daughter, yes. But who is the father?" Mr. Fawcett asked. "You don't see him about."

"Perhaps he's dead," Mr. Prentice suggested.

"I don't think so," Mr. Fawcett said dryly. Then he recollected the beginning of the conversation from whose point they had so far strayed. "So you discussed the lease with Paula? That sounds very likely," he went on sarcastically.

"She asked me much the same question as you have," Mr. Prentice assured him, "and I gave her much the same answer. I don't want to be curious, but would you mind telling me exactly who Iris is? I could, I suppose, find out quite easily by going to the Earl's solicitors and asking them point blank who the last tenant was. You see, as I had to accept the Earl's title, I did not see any abstract," he began to explain.

"I don't know what you're talking about," Mr. Fawcett interrupted him. "I'm sorry I ever brought up the subject at all," he went on, "only I was so certain that you would know where she had gone, that you'd be in touch with her over some business to do with the house." He gave Mr. Prentice another searching look, but seeing no response to his unasked question, shrugged his shoulders. "I made a mistake, that's all." Mr. Fawcett suddenly looked old and spent, and his eyes became wavering and uncertain. All the force of his fanaticism had vanished and in its place there flickered a fitful flame giving no heat and having no red centre. "Well, there it is," he added more to himself than to his host and began to walk towards the door as if he was unaware of the direction in which his footsteps were taking him.

Mr. Prentice watched him half way towards the passage before he realized that his unusual guest was leaving him. Jumping up, he laid a timid hand on his arm and Mr. Fawcett turned round and looked at him for a moment as if he had never seen him before. Then his eyes cleared and he carefully removed Mr. Prentice's hand with his own.

"You've been no help at all," he said in a flat voice.

"Why are you so worried about Iris and her whereabouts?" Mr. Prentice asked him gently. "And who exactly is she?" he went on.

Mr. Fawcett shook his head decisively; and Mr. Prentice noticed a tiny thread of fear weave its way across his face.

"It's no business of yours," Mr. Fawcett answered quickly. "None at all. It's all over and done with; you understand."

Before Mr. Prentice could press his point any more Mr. Fawcett had left the room at a surprising pace and, when Mr. Prentice reached the door of his study, he was only in time to see the front door close behind him. As it closed Markham appeared from the kitchen.

"I thought I heard the front door slam," he said. It was a very ordinary observation to make, but Mr. Prentice was instantly aware that Markham had not come out of his kitchen with his usual self-confidence.

Markham had always been very much at home in Mr. Prentice's flat in the Temple; he had greeted callers and strangers alike with assurance, and had left neither in doubt that he controlled their comings and goings. He had constituted himself the guard upon the gate and if, for some reason, the visitor could not make a proper impression upon him, it had needed Mr. Prentice's personal intervention to shepherd his guest past Cerberus.

This hesitant Markham was a person with whom Mr. Prentice was not at all familiar; nor did he understand the expression of relief that flitted across Markham's face the moment he had seen him standing in the passage. But before he had time to do more than note these differences from the ordinary, Markham became the servant he had always known.

"You're early," he said. "I thought I heard voices just then. Was anyone with you?"

"A gentleman by the name of Fawcett. I believe he lives at Number 5," Mr. Prentice replied.

"Oh, him!" Markham exclaimed with disgust. "He's a bible-puncher. He spent ten minutes this morning walking up and down the courtyard reading the Bible, and every now and again he'd stop and glare at this house. What's wrong with this house?"

Mr. Prentice visualized the lean Mr. Fawcett without much trouble.

"Nothing as far as I know," Mr. Prentice answered him emphatically, "but Mr. Fawcett is very concerned about the wickedness in the world," he said in a reproving voice.

"So am I," Markham answered, "but mumbling about with the Bible won't cure it; and staring at these windows as if this house contained it all is not what I like."

"I find it rather interesting," Mr. Prentice admitted. "Mr. Fawcett is obviously suffering from some very strong emotion and that concerns this house and its occupant."

"I've never met the man," Markham said indignantly.

"I should have said its former occupant," Mr. Prentice explained.

Markham's flood of indignation was suddenly stemmed, and it seemed to Mr. Prentice that his sad features became set in a sadder and more rigid mould than usual.

"Have you found out who she was?" he asked.

Mr. Prentice looked at him in some astonishment.

"I thought," he said, "that you weren't interested in your neighbours."

"She's hardly a neighbour," Markham remarked. "In any event it doesn't matter."

He turned away and went back into the kitchen, and Mr. Prentice returned to his study where he poured himself out a glass of sherry while Lottie Spate watched him with no great interest.

"I find Markham's behaviour rather odd," he said to the dog. "In fact, the only person who appears to be behaving rationally is yourself. What has frightened Markham? Something or someone has thrown him out of his usual circumspect stride. Who or what makes Mr. Fawcett perform his morning devotions in public? Why does Mr. Speed totter to drink the waters of Lethe in so deliberate a fashion? Why are the entertaining couple next door not really entertaining each other at all? And why"—he paused in his questions—"and why did I look round my own room last night as if I expected to find that an intruder had been?"

Lottie Spate, beyond a slight movement of the tail, made no other response to the questions, and Mr. Prentice resumed his seat in his armchair, a quiet smile playing about his puckered mouth. He had found himself thinking of the woman whom Mr. Fawcett had called "fallen". It was a description that he hadn't heard for many years; then he thought of the golden shaft of light that had enfiladed the Court on the previous night and of the expensive car whose departure he had heard; then he looked at Lottie Spate again and fell asleep.

He was awakened by a noise that for several seconds he could neither recognize nor locate; it sounded like a woodpecker and it appeared to be cutting glass. Eventually he turned his head towards the window where he saw the indistinct outline of a woman's figure, and discovered that the noise was being made by fingers rhythmically drumming on the leaded panes. Mr. Prentice, who should have felt a stab of annoyance at such an intrusion on his privacy, owned to himself as he went towards the window that he felt nothing of the kind. All he was really conscious of was an overwhelming sense of curiosity. Opening the window cautiously he found Joyce's face within a few inches of his own.

"I couldn't stand up to Markham again so soon," she explained. "He has a very discomfiting effect on me."

"You needn't," Mr. Prentice assured her. "I'll open the door for you myself."

"I wasn't really coming in," Joyce said hesitatingly. "I was only bringing back the fish knives and forks. I don't know whether they enjoyed the change of owners—I hope so."

Mr. Prentice took no notice of the parcel which she was handing out to him over the heads of his marigolds.

"I've still got plenty of sherry," he said, "and your presence will afford me an excuse to drink some more of it."

Leaving his study at what was almost a trot, he opened his front door to her with a flourish, noticing that once again Joyce paused at the entrance to his study and appeared to brace herself before she crossed the threshold. However, she was smiling at him when he joined her and appeared to be wholly at her ease again.

"I like this room of yours very much," she said. "It's friendly and dirty without being unclean, if you know what I mean."

"Markham has his standards," Mr. Prentice replied as he opened his corner cupboard and took out the decanter and two glasses. "But they are not perhaps as high as they should be. Still, they never vary and that is a very important thing." He put down the decanter on the table and went through the ritual of holding first one glass, and then the other to the light to see whether any dust lingered. "Mr. Fawcett was telling me a little while ago that there were no standards any longer, and that we were all slowly but surely being sucked under. The world was up to its chest in the morass and I gathered that very little, if anything, was being done to save it—except, of course, by Mr. Fawcett."

Joyce made a moue of disgust.

"So he called on you, did he? He's a lay preacher or something odd," she said, shaking her head so that her short fair hair danced and shimmered for a moment. "He called on Norman and myself when we were first married. Norman had the curious idea in those days that you didn't pay any attention to anyone who wasn't a prospective client. It took a minute to find out that Mr. Fawcett regarded money as the root of all evil and another minute to discover his very unflattering opinion about stockbrokers. Having failed to get Norman to give up his livelihood he was forced to turn his attention to me, and my unfortunate face and figure prompted him to try and save me." Joyce ran her hands down her hips and thighs. "He doesn't like natural lines, that man. Or does he? I don't know."

Mr. Prentice poured the sherry into the glasses with meticulous care; indeed, his whole attention seemed to be taken up with the performance, but that he was acutely aware of what she was saying was plain from his next remark though he took pains to keep his interest hidden.

"Do you think he really likes natural lines?" he asked. "I don't think myself that there is anything more beautiful than a beautiful woman."

"How very comforting you are," Joyce said, sitting down on the arm of his armchair.

Mr. Prentice gave her a small appreciative smile, handed her a glass of sherry and made a gesture of drinking her health as he sipped his own.

"I think Mr. Fawcett is probably part and parcel of one of the oldest stories in the world," he said. "He tries to exorcise the devil in others, but the devil dwells himself in Mr. Fawcett."

"How very hospitable of Mr. Fawcett!" Joyce exclaimed.

"My dear, he's a very unwelcome guest I should think," Mr. Prentice said. "But try as hard as he can I think that Mr. Fawcett signally fails to get rid of him. He has taken a long lease of his soul." He held his sherry up to the light, not to observe its colour, but to take the edge from his next question.

"And Mrs. Fawcett?" he asked.

"In a couple of years or so I've seen her once or twice," Joyce answered him without any reservations. "She looks rather like a moth, all dried up and thin and small and indeterminate and drab and pathetic. She flurries past you and never seems to change her dress, a pale grey cotton affair. I've only seen her on a Sunday, presumably on her way to church, with her husband stalking beside her looking like an eagle. The rabbit and the eagle."

Mr. Prentice took hold of the decanter and, poising it near Joyce's glass, waited for her to hold it out to him. When she did so and, as he poured the sherry carefully into it, he put another question.

"Do you think Mr. Fawcett called on Iris?" he asked.

He didn't look at Joyce as he asked the question, nor did he look at her glass, but his eyes were fixed upon the small, well-shaped hand that held it. He saw it tremble a moment, and then he saw the fingers grasp the stem tighter. There was a pause and he sensed that Joyce was staring at the liquid as he slowly refilled her glass.

"Iris?" she repeated at length, but the languid friendly note had slipped away from her voice and hidden itself behind a granite façade. "I haven't the least idea," she went on almost harshly. "I expect so," she added perfunctorily. "I oughtn't to be having another glass. I should be getting back," she went on hurriedly, rising to her feet.

Mr. Prentice put down the decanter in haste.

"Oh, please don't go yet," he urged her. "It's quite early unless, of course, your husband will be getting impatient. By the way, what is his name?"

Joyce opened her grey eyes wide with surprise and appeared to have forgone momentarily her intention to leave at once.

"Norman, of course," she answered.

"His surname, I mean."

"Oh, I forgot, we've never been formally introduced. Though there's nothing very unusual in that in these days, is there?"

Mr. Prentice thought her answer rather breathlessly delivered for her.

"Cumming," Joyce continued. "Norman Richard Cumming."

"My name's Prentice," Mr. Prentice said.

"I don't think the world's changed," Joyce remarked.

"Since when?" Mr. Prentice asked very puzzled.

"Since we knew each other's surnames. It's just part of a game called civilization, isn't it?" Joyce replied. There was a bitter edge to her voice and Mr. Prentice noticed that her small rounded chin appeared suddenly very sharp, and in her eyes there flared a rebellious flame.

"You're dissatisfied with the present state of intellectual and moral development?" Mr. Prentice suggested.

"I don't think there has been any so far as human relations are concerned," Joyce replied.

"You can't really mean that," Mr. Prentice began, but Joyce waved him to silence.

"Pay no attention to me," she interrupted him. "I don't know anything about it anyway. But there are times when life is bloody, and times when it's very bloody. At present it's——" she stopped abruptly, put down the remainder of her sherry at a gulp and smiled at Mr. Prentice gravely and without humour. "I imagine that will be enough of life for one evening and, as I told you before I think, I don't bother about the future." She gave a challenging toss of her head, but her eyes fell before the look of disbelief in the mild gaze of Mr. Prentice. Then she went almost hurriedly to the door where she turned and watched him as he ambled after her, anxious to see her politely off the premises.

"I never thanked you for returning my ring," she said. "I should and do."

Mr. Prentice was quite astonished at his own lapse of memory; he had never given a thought to the matter since Joyce's arrival. Automatically his eyes swept over her hand and he noticed that, though she had received it, she was not wearing it.

"It was lucky I saw it," he answered hurriedly.

"So it was you," Joyce said. "I guessed it must be because of the envelope." She walked hurriedly down the hall with Mr. Prentice in her wake.

"Remember me to your husband," he blurted out when he had grasped the handle of the front door and she had slid out before he had thought the door was opened wide enough to allow the departure of a cat, much less of a human being. His final remark, however, halted her hasty steps and she spun round to give him the benefit of her most dazzling smile. Suddenly Mr. Prentice realized that she was not merely a pretty woman; she was a very pretty woman indeed.

"When I see him again, I will," she answered. "And if by any chance you see him first, you might remember me to him." Joyce began to whistle gently to herself as she watched him with a pair of amused eyes.

"He's gone away?" Mr. Prentice said blankly.

"Chasing a wild goose," Joyce answered.

Still whistling softly she turned away from him and, entering her own house, shut the door unmistakably behind her.

For a moment Mr. Prentice stared after her, then looked guiltily round him to see whether he had been discovered, but the court was still hot in the evening of the day and empty. He went back into his own house, shutting the door very quietly and, coming again into his study and picking up his half-full glass of sherry, found himself humming the tune that Joyce had whistled. Although he knew it very well he could not think what it was called. Carrying his glass with him he went through into the kitchen with the parcel of fish knives and forks in search of Markham.

Having found him and handed over the case he hummed the tune a little louder and asked Markham if he knew what it was. Markham looked at him in pity at his ignorance.

"You ought to know," he said. "We heard it often enough when we were in the Temple."

"Perhaps, but what is it?"

"It's a hymn, 'O Perfect Love'," Markham replied, disgust replacing pity in his expression.

"Of course—'O Perfect Love all human thought transcending,'" Mr. Prentice repeated, turning back again with his sherry glass in his hand. "I don't like cynicism in women," he murmured to himself. "They should laugh or cry, but not be bitter. It's very odd how I came to forget all about the ring. I suppose all the time I was talking to Mrs. Cumming I must have been thinking of someone else."

He re-entered his study and remained standing in the middle of the room with a puzzled frown on his chubby face. What had been a strange tiny cloud on his horizon and noticeable simply because the rest of the sky had been so familiar, had now been augmented by others until a large part of his "inverted bowl" was overcast. It was really beginning to exasperate him the way in which, whenever he brought up the subject of the late lessee of his house, he found himself pulled up short. Mrs. Cumming appeared to be willing to talk quite freely about anyone else. Mr. Fawcett and Mr. Speed had contributed only negative evidence; but by their evasions they had all three whetted his appetite; and his hunger was increasing every hour. Many another man would never have bothered his head about the matter at all and many another, even if his curiosity had been aroused, would have laid it to rest at the first rebuff; but Mr. Prentice had spent all his life untying knots and had never been in the habit of cutting the string. This had seemed such a simple knot, too. It probably was a simple one; but it was just that his fingers were all thumbs. All the same he was determined to find out who Iris was and why she had left St. Anne's Court.

When Markham brought him his coffee after dinner he found Mr. Prentice and Lottie Spate engaged in a game of question and answer—not that Lottie Spate was doing anything but cast a pair of intelligent eyes at her master who, pencil in hand, was asking himself questions aloud and setting down the answers beside them. But in spite of having covered the best part of a sheet of notepaper, Mr. Prentice was back where he had started and the question that he was putting to Lottie Spate when Markham entered with his coffee was the old one.

"Who was Iris?" he asked Lottie Spate.

Markham put down the tray.

"Do you mean Lady Iris Todhunter?" Markham asked him.

Mr. Prentice laid down his pencil with great deliberation on the table and gave his whole attention to Markham.

"If that is the name of the lady who vacated this house before we arrived, I do," Mr. Prentice replied.

"Well, it was," Markham said and was about to leave the room without any further ado when Mr. Prentice held up his hand.

"Wait a moment, Markham," he interposed. "How did you find this out, and why?"

"I went to the post office. They ended by being quite obliging." He stopped abruptly and again made an effort to leave the study, but Mr. Prentice once more interrupted him.

"That is the how," he said. "What of the why?"

Markham did not answer his question immediately; it appeared to his master that he was considering what reply he should give and Mr. Prentice was fairly certain that when he did give one it wouldn't be the truth.

"I thought," Mr. Prentice went on softly, "that you weren't interested in any of your neighbours."

"I'm not," answered Markham promptly. "Anyway, Lady Iris is hardly a neighbour. Not that I'm interested in her; I thought you were," he finished a little defiantly. "In fact, when I came in with the coffee you were asking the question off the dog.

"Was I?" said Mr. Prentice. "But when you went to the post office I don't think I had——" he paused and picked up the pencil again, tapping it gently on the table. "Did you ask the official where she had gone as well?" he ended on a light note as if the answer was of no possible importance to him. Markham hesitated once more, this time palpably, and Mr. Prentice watched him curiously as he weighed his answer in the balance. "Truth has a singularly plain face," Mr. Prentice murmured, looking at Lottie Spate. "She is not, for instance, as good-looking as you, Miss Spate; but she is wholesome and, if you embrace her, you at any rate know that her lipstick won't come away on your mouth or her powder on your sleeve."

"As a matter of fact, I did ask where she had gone,"

Markham replied at length. "They wouldn't tell me. She'd left a forwarding address, they said, and letters would be sent on." Once he had decided to acknowledge his curiosity Markham finished almost with a rush of words to the mouth. "Apparently a forwarding address is confidential; same as if you don't put your number in the telephone book," he explained.

"You appear to have gone to a considerable amount of trouble in this matter," Mr. Prentice put in. "Were you still imbued with the noble idea of helping me?"

"Of course," Markham answered after another slight pause. "You don't suppose I'm interested, do you?"

"No, no, certainly not," Mr. Prentice replied hurriedly.

"That's all right then," Markham said and this time he did succeed in reaching the door and quitting the room before Mr. Prentice was able to interpose any further barrier. But if he was under any impression that he had disabused his master's mind of any suspicion that his enquiries were entirely his own affair, Markham was very much mistaken, because no sooner had he gone than Mr. Prentice filled in the name of Lady Iris Todhunter against his ultimate question, and then proceeded to put down a couple more. "Why did Markham want to know who she was? And where she had gone?"

From his long association with his servant, Mr. Prentice was only too well aware that Markham neither suffered from, nor encouraged in others, any form of curiosity. He was that veritable Englishman who was quite convinced that his birthright and his own business were more important than anything else and were quite sufficient for his own needs. This interest of his, therefore, in a person who was a complete stranger to him was a very remarkable thing, and Mr. Prentice did not fail to remark it. It was so much nonsense to try and make out that he had merely been fulfilling his master's wishes. Normally he would have done nothing about them because he would have considered that it was a vulgar proceeding and would have ignored his master's interest altogether.

Something must, therefore, have happened that had shaken the sad and solitary figure of Markham out of its usual apathy, and Mr. Prentice was nearly positive that whatever it was that had such a powerful effect, it was not the behaviour of Mr. Fawcett nor his wife, nor Mr. Speed, nor the young couple next door, nor the mother and child opposite. Their behaviour had, in one way or another, influenced Mr. Prentice, but it was something or someone outside their neighbours that had reacted so palpably upon Markham.

Mr. Prentice ran his hand through his sparse hair; it was so absurd that he should find his mind crowded with a problem which was probably no problem at all, and in any event he did not know why he was bothering his head about the matter. Lady Iris was nothing to him; "Less than the dust" he began to hum to himself, and probably would never acquire any greater stature. Yet, even while he tossed the enigma away, he could not keep his thoughts from ranging about her unsubstantial person.

Did she walk a shepherdess of sheep? Or was she crossing the road in her latest new bonnet? Or did she walk like Chloris alone? Was she dark? Was she fair? Was she short? Was she tall? Mr. Prentice put the unending questions to himself and supplied the answers that he liked best. It was a game that he enjoyed playing; so, he had heard, did the great thinkers in Tibet conjure up their ladies; but though his imagination wrought a dream of a fair woman Mr. Prentice could not make her materialize; but it was not for want of trying and so intent did he become that he was unaware that his door had opened and that Markham was standing in the entrance, looking at him with a strange and anxious expression on his face.

Indeed, it took Mr. Prentice some seconds to focus Markham's body, but gradually his own figment was dispelled and slowly his servant's corporal entity replaced it.

"What is it?" Mr. Prentice asked him in sharper tones than he meant to use.

"I thought—I wondered," Markham stammered. "Can you hear anyone crying?" he finished.

"Crying?" Mr. Prentice repeated, not taking his eyes from Markham's face which was still overcast by an expression of anxiety. "Yes, I think I can," he went on, getting up from his chair and going to the window. The moment he unlatched it the noise became at once recognizable. "It's that child again," he finished.

"So it is," Markham replied. "I thought——" he began again and then changed the course of his conversation abruptly. "I wish she'd keep the child quiet," he grumbled and turned on his heel. Mr. Prentice hesitated a moment and then, after closing the window, opened the front door and stepped quietly out into the courtyard. It was nearly dark and the fat trunk and the slender arms of the ash tree looked very black against the evening sky. Mr. Prentice stood a moment watching the uneasy swaying of the branches and thinking about Markham's odd behaviour. Who did he imagine was crying if not Paula?

"Her mother must be out," Mr. Prentice muttered to himself and, tiptoeing over to the door of Number 1, remained standing outside it in a somewhat helpless fashion while Lottie Spate, who had followed him out, inspected the bottom of the ash tree and the child sobbed miserably above him. Eventually he put out a hand to ring the bell and then withdrew it again hastily, thinking Paula might be frightened. Then he stood a little way away from the door and, making a funnel with his hands, called to her gently at first and then, after she had taken no notice, a little louder.

"Paula! Paula!"

Suddenly the cries stopped and, as Mr. Prentice stood in the court, he thought he saw the curtains move in one of the upper rooms, but no one spoke to him.

"I'll come in and talk to you if you like," he said, and he was still looking up at the curtained windows when he became aware that Lottie Spate had left the ash tree and was in front of him watching the front door which was opened a foot, and through the gap a sliver of light shone steadfastly out. Mr. Prentice moved forward and pushing the door farther open saw a small figure clad in a nightdress, standing in the hallway. Lottie Spate advanced confidently wagging her tail and Mr. Prentice followed in her wake, closing the door behind him.

"You must turn the light off," Paula informed him. "Mother always makes me do that."

"And you must go back to bed," Mr. Prentice whispered, though why he hadn't spoken in his ordinary voice he hadn't any idea. "I'll come up with you for a moment if you like."

Apparently Paula did like because without saying a word she began to mount the stairs, leaving Mr. Prentice and his dog to follow her. When they reached the top she turned into a room which corresponded to that of Markham's in Number 6 and, after she had turned off the stair light, climbed back into bed where she awaited her visitors. Mr. Prentice, followed by Lottie Spate, came gingerly into the room.

"Now tell me a story," Paula said. "Like Iris used to do."

Mr. Prentice sat down on the end of her bed and, noticing that the window was open, shut it carefully.

"So Iris used to tell you stories, did she?" he replied.

"If I cried," Paula said.

"But you mustn't cry. Big girls like you don't cry."

"Oh yes, they do," Paula contradicted him with assurance. "Why, I've seen mother cry and Iris and—oh lots of people!" She settled her small body in the bed and, putting her fair head upon the pillow, looked at Mr. Prentice with tear-stained blue eyes. "Tell me a story about your dog," she said.

"First you tell me something," Mr. Prentice replied. "Did Iris come here often?"

Paula nodded.

"But that's a secret," she said. "If I woke," she went on in a swift confidential tone, "and mother was out, I'd pretend to cry and then Iris would come over and tell me a story."

"I expect Iris was out sometimes."

Paula nodded again in agreement.

"And then I'd go to sleep," she said.

"And what was Iris like?" Mr. Prentice asked.

"She was good," Paula said and went on with a rush of words. "I used to go to her house a lot, but mother stopped me. She said Iris didn't want to see me; but it wasn't true, was it?"

Mr. Prentice found himself a little uncomfortable, perched as he was on the horns of this dilemma, and hastily avoided the question.

"I mean what did she look like?" he asked.

"She looked like a lady, of course," Paula said.

"Yes, but was she dark or fair or——" Mr. Prentice began.

"She was very nice," Paula interrupted. "I liked her much better than mother."

"I don't think you ought to say things like that," Mr. Prentice said doubtfully.

"Tell me a story," Paula urged him and her wide eyes looked into his with confidence. They had arrived, Mr. Prentice felt, at the testing moment and he cast around for a tale.

"Once upon a time," Mr. Prentice began, "there lived in a house very like this——"

"With pink silk curtains?" Paula interrupted. "Mother's room has pink."

"Has it?" said Mr. Prentice politely, but shuddering inwardly. "No, this house had blue curtains."

"I like blue," Paula said.

"That's splendid then," Mr. Prentice answered. "And in this house there lived alone a very beautiful princess," he went on.

"Princesses live in castles," Paula announced.

"They don't now," Mr. Prentice assured her. "At any rate this one didn't," he went on hastily. "And she was tall and fair and her name was Iris."

"Was it really?" Paula asked.

Mr. Prentice nodded a solemn assurance.

"And had she violet eyes like Iris?" Paula asked.

Mr. Prentice nodded again.

"And did she have blue brushes?"

"Blue brushes!" Mr. Prentice exclaimed.

"The backs were blue," Paula explained.

"Oh yes," said Mr. Prentice very relieved.

"And did she sing?"

"All day," Mr. Prentice answered confidently. "Because she was very happy because she had fallen in love with a prince."

"What was the prince like?" Paula asked.

Mr. Prentice looked at her.

"Well," he said, very confidentially, "I'm not much of a hand at describing men. I thought you'd be able to tell me about the prince."

"Well, there's Toddy, of course," Paula replied, "but he's more of a friend of mother's."

"Toddy!" Mr. Prentice echoed the name in surprise.

"I expect mother's having dinner with him to-night," Paula said. "She generally does."

"What's he like?" Mr. Prentice asked.

"Well, he's rather tall and he's generally laughing; but I don't know him very well," Paula answered. "He's always so late."

"Is he a friend of Iris?" Mr. Prentice asked.

"I saw him there once, but he's always here," Paula said and her eyes seemed to Mr. Prentice to be not nearly so large; indeed, the lids kept on falling and rising again with more and more difficulty.

"One day," Mr. Prentice went on, "the princess looked out of her window and she saw the prince talking to someone else, and she didn't like——" he stopped abruptly as he saw that Paula was asleep. Then rising gently, he opened the window again softly and, beckoning to Lottie Spate, prepared to put out the light and leave the room. It was then that he became aware that he was not alone with the little girl. Through the door he heard faint whispers and, on opening it not without a little trepidation, he found himself confronted by a young man, who was coatless and whose braces dangled about his legs and who was holding a heavy bronze vase in his hand. Behind him he saw a woman in a peignoir who looked every bit as frightened as he felt. Mr. Prentice put his fingers to his lips to enjoin silence and, after he had closed the door, began to descend the stairs followed by a subdued dog. In his wake came the young man, still holding the vase, and a little time after him the woman. When they reached the hall the young man took him firmly by the arm and Mr. Prentice found himself in the sitting-room.

"What's the idea?" asked the young man. "Suppose you turn out your pockets for a start."

"Don't be ridiculous, Toddy," the woman broke out as she entered the room. Her voice was pleasant and Mr. Prentice, who had kept his eyes on the bronze vase, now raised them to hers. He saw a medium sized person of plump appearance whose short hair was startlingly light, and whose face was very carefully tended against the strains and stresses of either the onslaught of the years or the weather. Mr. Prentice judged her to be no longer very young, but he thought she was no more than thirty. As their eyes met Mr. Prentice saw what he imagined to be a glint of humour in hers. "Now that I can see this gentleman properly, I'm perfectly certain I've seen him before. Anyway, burglary with a spaniel would be very odd. And for God's sake don't make a noise! Paula is asleep."

Mr. Prentice on hearing the young man addressed as Toddy took much more interest in him. He was a loose limbed, indeterminate kind of youth who appeared to be amiable, if weak, and by his clothes, or those of them which he was still wearing, Mr. Prentice judged him to be in easy circumstances.

"My name is Prentice," he said to her. "And I live in Number 6."

"I saw you last night; I remember now, trying to hold up my next door neighbour," she replied. "Had you had a good evening?"

"I only met him in the courtyard," Mr. Prentice explained hastily.

"Toddy, you look ridiculous," the woman said suddenly. "Put down that wretched vase and you'd better"— she hesitated a fraction of a second—"go upstairs," she continued firmly, "and put your coat on. And don't forget your braces are hanging down and go quietly."

The young man looked from one to the other.

"If you think you'll be safe," he began doubtfully.

"I'll be safe enough," she interrupted him a trifle grimly. "The only thing I can possibly lose, which is my reputation, I've lost already." She sighed and gave Mr. Prentice a fleeting smile. "However, that's nothing new around here."

The young man put down the vase very carefully and, after throwing a backward glance at the uncomfortable Mr. Prentice, went slowly out, his braces dangling behind him like a pair of useless reins. The moment he had gone the woman gave Mr. Prentice a cheerful, if slightly impudent, smile and pointing to a chair waited for him to sit down. Mr. Prentice, feeling that his presence was quite superfluous, cast a despairing glance towards the door, but as the woman seated herself on the sofa he saw no other alternative but to sit down himself. This he did on the very edge of the chair, looking and feeling somewhat ridiculous.

"Now, Mr. Prentice," the woman began in a light and friendly tone of voice, "perhaps you wouldn't mind explaining exactly what you were doing in my house. Incidentally, you were so quiet about it that I shouldn't have known you were here at all, if I hadn't seen the light under Paula's door when I went into the passage to turn off the light there and heard you speaking."

"Paula was crying," Mr. Prentice explained. "My servant—I heard her. I thought perhaps if I could get into the house I might manage to get her to go to sleep. Not that I've any experience with children," he went on hastily, "but we had met and, of course, I'd no idea that you would be back so soon, Mrs. —er——" he paused expectantly.

"Mrs. Dawson," the woman helped him out. "I think that was very kind of you," she continued. "Paula told me she had met you, but I told her not to bother you. One's own children are quite enough of a trial without having to bother with other people's." She sighed again and offered him a cigarette from the box on the table. "I find it very difficult to keep the child out of mischief all the day long. I'll have to send her to a day school, or something."

Mr. Prentice declined the cigarette and, while she lit one herself, began to feel a little more at ease as he shifted himself from the edge of the chair on to the seat.

"I suppose Lady Iris was a great deal of help," he put in tentatively.

The words were spoken quietly with no emphasis; they were thrown away casually, but Mr. Prentice realized at once that he had aroused antagonism where before he had met only goodwill. The smile left Mrs. Dawson's face and her eyes became hard and unsympathetic, but the reply which hovered on her lips remained for the moment undelivered because Toddy, returning to the room, echoed the name and the remark himself.

"Iris?" he asked. "When was she a great deal of help?"

"I was just about to explain to Mrs. Dawson," Mr. Prentice replied hastily, "that Paula has told me that Lady Iris——"

"Yes, we know all about that," Mrs. Dawson interrupted brusquely. "And now I think you'd better be going, Toddy."

The young man looked slightly taken aback at receiving his dismissal so summarily, but he didn't protest as Mrs. Dawson jumped up from the sofa and, taking him by the arm, practically pushed him from the room, shutting the door after them so that Mr. Prentice couldn't hear their goodbyes.

Alone, he looked round the room which he saw to be shoddily furnished with a few pieces of very ordinary furniture, the upholstery of which would have benefited from a few minor repairs and a major cleaning. There were no photographs, but one or two coloured prints of no merit were dotted on the walls. There was no clock and Mr. Prentice, pulling out his watch, saw to his astonishment that it was only half-past ten. As he was putting it away Mrs. Dawson returned. Mr. Prentice rose to his feet and began to make for the door.

"You mustn't go yet," Mrs. Dawson said and he saw that she had recovered her good temper. "I've sent Toddy home and I'm going to get you a drink for all your trouble." Before he had time either to accept or refuse she had walked out of the room across the passage and returned with a syphon, a decanter of whisky and two glasses on a tray. She didn't ask him how much whisky he wanted, but poured out a very generous measure for him and much less for herself.

"I'm really very grateful to you," she said, after squirting in the soda water, as she handed him his glass and resettled herself on the sofa. "Paula is another thing the neighbours have started to complain about. This time I gather it's the man from Number 2. They are all so damned selfish they won't have any children themselves, and on the top of it they complain about Paula."

"Another thing?" Mr. Prentice echoed her.

"That extraordinary creature, Fawcett, has already written twice to the Earl's solicitors accusing me of keeping a brothel here," she replied lightly.

"And are you?" asked Mr. Prentice. "I only ask out of curiosity's sake," he went on quickly. "I've never been in a brothel."

"Neither have I," said Mrs. Dawson.

"Who lives in Number 2?" Mr. Prentice asked hastily. "I don't know him. In fact, I've never seen him."

"And I don't suppose you will," she said. "He lives alone and he seems to come and go at all hours. He's very quiet; not like our friend next door. He hasn't been here long—six months, I should say. I've only seen him once or twice myself; a thinnish energetic person of about thirty-five or so; but he's always complaining about the noise. Says it interferes with his work." She took a sip of her whisky and looked Mr. Prentice over very carefully.

"What do you do, or are you a gentleman of leisure?" she asked.

"I'm a barrister. Rather dull, I'm afraid. You see, I deal with wills and land and things like that," Mr. Prentice hastily went on to forestall any questions about the criminal or the divorce courts about which women appeared to him to display an inordinate interest.

"Land." Mrs. Dawson repeated the word rather uncertainly as if she did not quite know what he meant.

"People are always fighting over land," Mr. Prentice said airily and, unwilling to enter into a description of Chancery practice, changed the subject with some violence. "Do you know the Cummings?" he asked.

Mrs. Dawson laughed; there was no bitterness in it, there was even a certain jollity about it.

"I know who you mean; the pretty girl across the way and her not too bad-looking husband," she said. "But you should get into your head, Mr. Prentice," she went on, leaning forward to emphasize her remarks, "that I am not a *persona grata* here. I don't know anyone really except poor Jim Speed."

"Are you implying——" Mr. Prentice began.

"I'm not implying anything," Mrs. Dawson interrupted him. "I am stating a fact, and I am not complaining. Some people are wise and sad, some people are foolish and glad; but very few are glad and wise."

"You've left out the foolish and sad," Mr. Prentice reminded her.

"They're in the great majority," she admitted. "I suppose I am in that bunch. And yet"—she screwed up her eyes as if to lengthen her vision—"and yet I don't know. I wouldn't be upset at all if it wasn't for that Fawcett creature. If he thinks he can drive me away from here he's very much mistaken."

"Action can't be taken against you just because you have a lover," Mr. Prentice observed, thinking to put her at her ease by accepting the situation in which he had found himself without embarrassment. "As a matter of fact, in one way you're very fortunate," he declared with a certain amount of enthusiasm.

"Fortunate!"

"So many women never have one," Mr. Prentice explained.

"Oddly enough I am very much in favour of marriage," she said. "But marriage doesn't seem to be in favour of me."

Mr. Prentice looked at her keenly and his mild eyes became a little shrewd. He hadn't understood her last remark at all.

"I thought your husband was dead or that perhaps——" he stopped.

"Hasn't Mr. Fawcett called on you yet?" she asked him, a malicious smile curving about her lips.

"Oh yes."

"And didn't he tell you all my history or what he knows of it, which is somewhat different?" she went on.

"He did imply that you weren't all that you should be," Mr. Prentice admitted a little uncomfortably.

Mrs. Dawson sipped her whisky and soda for a moment in silence; it seemed to Mr. Prentice that he was being put on the scales and weighed. When she spoke again he knew the balance had been favourable.

"I expect he'll tell you some time," she said at length and shrugged her shoulders as if the matter was' of small importance. "He went home to his own country and never married me. He was married already. It was just one of those things, you know. The war was on then, and so was life and death. One was foolish and now one's sad. Although I'm not certain about the sadness." She looked at him rather solemnly. "But it was terrific while it lasted," she added, "and nothing's been the same since."

Mr. Prentice reflected a moment on the tragic little story and on what he thought to be the strange behaviour of womenkind in general, and Mrs. Dawson in particular. Then, as he felt himself becoming weak and full of tears, he cleared his throat in monstrous fashion and took an enormous swallow of his drink.

"You ought to marry," he announced, but Mrs. Dawson shook her head slowly from side to side.

"I haven't loved any man, except one, sufficiently to marry him," she replied. "And I don't think it probable I ever shall. I like men though, and they like me as a rule, and one way and another I've had a lot of experience of them since— in the last three or four years. Besides which," she finished with a smile, "someone has got to pay the bills. He's got a wife and children, and in any case I don't know where the hell he's got to now."

Mr. Prentice looked round the sitting-room, more with the idea of avoiding her eyes in which he felt sure a certain agony was showing, but which as a matter of fact showed no sign of self pity, than because he wanted to study the furnishings again.

"And life's expensive here," he murmured.

"It is," she agreed, "but I like St. Anne's Court and Paula was born here—that's why Mr. Fawcett knows so much— he and I are the oldest inhabitants—and I can't bring myself to leave everything behind when there is nothing to replace it. But barristers make a lot of money, don't they?" She switched the conversation away from herself in an effortless and easy manner.

"Some of them do," Mr. Prentice admitted. "I don't manage so badly myself, but I'm afraid I shall have to do a little better if I'm going to stay here for any length of time. And I do want to do just that." He smiled to himself. "It's a queer thing, but I've always wanted to live in a place like this. I used to live in the Temple; that's the next best thing, I suppose."

She looked at him and laughed gently.

"You look prosperous enough," she said. "A nice round stomach, a chubby face and a baldish head."

Mr. Prentice ran his hand the length of his head and smiled a little ruefully.

"Looks don't mean everything," he said. "It's a state of mind that makes for the appearance of ease and success. You, for instance, have been born with it, or acquired it. No one would guess your history from your face; you don't let life bewilder you or overwhelm you. I am the same. I don't remember ever having worried about anything, although I must admit I'm worried now a little." He gave her a sidelong glance. "And the stupid thing is that it has all got nothing to do with me personally, and I really don't know why the whole thing keeps popping in and out of my mind."

"What is it all about?" Mrs. Dawson asked him in the polite, cool tones of a nurse who is trying to solace a fractious patient.

"It's about someone you don't like," Mr. Prentice answered her.

"I shouldn't let Mr. Fawcett's threat of hell trouble you," she replied. "Everyone he consigns there ain't goin' there," she parodied.

"He may even find himself there," Mr. Prentice said. "No, it's not Mr. Fawcett. I wonder whether you'd care to tell me why you dislike Lady Iris." He put the question directly to her and then hastily averted his eyes. But Mrs. Dawson only, for the moment, showed astonishment.

"You too!" she exclaimed. "Where did you meet her?"

"I haven't," Mr. Prentice said hurriedly. "I don't know her at all. I don't even know what she looks like."

"Then what on earth——" Mrs. Dawson began.

"Paula is really at the bottom of the whole business," Mr. Prentice interrupted her. "She, so to speak, started my mind worrying and I have been worrying ever since because no one will answer my questions."

"What do you want to know?" she asked him quietly.

"Why she went and where she is," Mr. Prentice answered her. "And why you dislike her," he added.

Mrs. Dawson raised her eyebrows.

"You don't want to know much, do you?" she said a little sarcastically. "I can't really see that any of this is of the slightest importance, and I don't care for curiosity much, and certainly not casual curiosity."

"I don't like it myself," Mr. Prentice admitted. "I am not a curious man. I don't really know why I am being so inquisitive; I don't think that I should have thought about her again if Mr. or Mrs. Cumming, or Mr. Speed, or even Mr. Fawcett had been straightforward, but none of them was. Why are they all so secretive?"

"So you've been trying to pump everyone," Mrs. Dawson said, but there was no malice in her voice, only a tinge of amusement. "Well, I'll tell you why I dislike her if you like, but after I've done so I should let matters drop if I were you. What are those lines of Browning's: 'Where the apple reddens never pry'——" She stopped and frowned in her effort to remember the rest of the couplet.

"'Lest we lose our Edens, you and I'," Mr. Prentice finished it for her. Mrs. Dawson nodded her acknowledgment.

"Lady Iris Todhunter is her full name," she said. "And she's the daughter of the Earl of Rawton."

"Ah!" Mr. Prentice exclaimed in satisfaction. "I didn't appreciate the fact that she was Lord Rawton's daughter. That accounts for it."

"Accounts for what?"

"Why she had the house in the first place," he replied.

"Like everything else it was handed to her on a platter,

if that's what you mean," Mrs. Dawson replied, a certain bitterness in her voice. "I don't know why she went, but I can make a guess, though I am not going to do so."

"She went very suddenly, didn't she?" Mr. Prentice asked.

"I suppose she did," Mrs. Dawson replied. "I was rather glad to see her go and so, I expect, was someone else," she added enigmatically. "As to where she is now," she went on quickly, "I haven't the faintest idea."

"I thought perhaps she might have written to Paula," Mr. Prentice suggested.

"Well, she hasn't," Mrs. Dawson replied sharply. "And I don't think she will."

"Paula was very fond of her?" Mr. Prentice tried again.

"Much too fond," Mrs. Dawson answered brusquely. "She began to monopolise her. I was put in second place."

"And that is why you dislike her," Mr. Prentice said.

"Largely," Mrs. Dawson admitted. "When a woman has lost as much as I have—in fact, when she has left only one thing worth having, she's not going to lose that —to a woman anyway. I can't stay at home all the time," she went on, "and I can't take Paula with me all the time." She shrugged her shoulders. "One can't expect children to disentangle values," she went on. "Naturally she thought the more of Iris and the less of me in proportion to the gifts and general spoiling that Iris gave her."

"Perhaps she was sorry for her," Mr. Prentice suggested.

"Perhaps she was, though for no reason," Mrs. Dawson replied. "All she did was to make the child discontented. Paula never used to lie awake and cry like this. She only did it to get Iris to come over, provided Iris was in. A little bit more of it and I shouldn't have had any control over my own child at all."

"Haven't you been unreasonably jealous?" Mr. Prentice asked her.

For a moment he thought that she was going to make an outburst, but after she had looked at him and found his expression to be mild and courteous, she threw up her hands in mock despair.

"I believe the trouble with you is that you are a romantic," she said. "You fashion women to suit your own ideas of them. The majority of them are not in the least what you think they are. Iris had what she thought was a good reason for her behaviour; but it wasn't love for Paula."

"What was it then?"

Mrs. Dawson shook her head very decidedly.

"I don't think I can go into that," she said. "In any case it is all over now so far as Iris is concerned. She has gone and I couldn't be more pleased." She rose to her feet and Mr. Prentice, taking the hint, got to his. Looking round for his dog he saw her curled up in the corner. Flicking his fingers he called her.

"Come on, Lottie Spate," he said. "Mrs. Dawson's had enough of us."

Mrs. Dawson looked at him with a mixture of disbelief and amusement.

"What did you call your dog?" she asked.

"Lottie Spate." Mr. Prentice admitted the name with a certain show of embarrassment.

"But why?" she persisted.

"Oh, it wouldn't mean anything to you," Mr. Prentice temporised.

Mrs. Dawson looked at him and impish laughter played in her eyes.

"She was a musical comedy actress, wasn't she?" she asked.

"Before your time," Mr. Prentice replied, weaving his way slowly but with purpose towards the door.

"One of your old flames?" Mrs. Dawson persisted again.

Mr. Prentice came to a halt while his dog waited expectantly at the door.

"Oh no," he said hurriedly. "I only worshipped from afar. I think she was the prettiest woman I've ever seen," he went on with great emphasis. "And I do so like to see pretty women —like you, for instance."

Mrs. Dawson gave him a brilliant smile.

"You have a great capacity for making me feel on good terms with myself," she said.

"I called my dog Lottie Spate because her coat reminded me of her hair and she's got very nice eyes too, don't you think? And she wriggles, too, very genteelly. Just as Miss Spate used to do."

"So you admired her red hair," Mrs. Dawson said. "I suppose it was real," she added lightly.

Mr. Prentice shook his head sadly.

"You're like my servant, Markham; he always suspects the truth. Of course it was real," he finished with confidence.

"I don't see how you could possibly know," Mrs. Dawson began. "As I said before you're just an incurable romantic," she went on, but what further she was going to say was interrupted by the loud and prolonged ringing of the front door bell. For the moment even Mrs. Dawson's self-confidence was shaken and she stood indecisively in the middle of the floor.

"I told Toddy not to come back," she whispered. "In any case he has a key," she murmured, more to herself than to Mr. Prentice who was wishing that he hadn't stayed quite so long. Another long and insistent ringing galvanized Mrs. Dawson into action.

"You'd better stay in here," she said to him as she swept out into the hall and opened the door so suddenly that the man who had been leaning not only on the bell, but on the panels, fell rather than walked into the hall. Mrs. Dawson hastily closed the door behind her.

"Jimmie," she said severely, "you're tight."

Mr. Speed reached the perpendicular again with some little difficulty.

"Nonsense!" he ejaculated. "Complete bosh."

"I think I'll be going now," Mr. Prentice said timidly, emerging into the hall.

"Perhaps you'll take Mr. Speed with you; you have met I believe," Mrs. Dawson said.

Mr. Prentice prepared to advance, but as Mr. Speed paid no attention to him whatever, he remained standing where he was while Mr. Speed, levering his enormous bulk nearer to Mrs. Dawson, leaned over her and dropped his voice to what he imagined to be a confidential level.

"It's time you and I had a little talk, Violette," he said.

Mrs. Dawson pursed her lips together and, drawing herself up, shook her head.

"No, Jimmie, not now or at any time," she replied.

"Don't be absurd," Mr. Speed began, but Mrs. Dawson interrupted him.

"I'm sorry for you, Jimmie," she said gently. "Don't think I'm not. Still, there are plenty of other fish in the sea."

"But I've decided now that I made an error—a gross error," he pleaded with her.

"It's no use your thinking that because Iris has left you high and dry—at least I suspect she has—that you can come round here," Mrs. Dawson said. "It's an old story," she went on with bitterness in her voice, "and old stories aren't very interesting. Now run along with Mr. Prentice or you'll wake up that child of mine."

Mr. Speed remained looking at her and for a moment seemed to be bereft of words; in the ensuing pause Mr. Prentice made his way gingerly towards the front door.

"Thank you for my pleasant drink," he said.

Mrs. Dawson held out her hand to him.

"Thank you for your help," she answered. "I like you and I am very attracted to Lottie Spate." She bent down to pat the dog. "Her red hair is real enough, anyway."

"I don't know whether——" Mr. Prentice began uncertainly. "Perhaps you'll allow——" he began again. "If it's any use to you and Mr.—er—Toddy," he blurted out at length, "I shall always be pleased to see Paula, especially on Saturday or Sunday afternoons; but perhaps you wouldn't care to——"

Mrs. Dawson put her hand upon his arm and gave it a gentle squeeze.

"And any time you want a glass of sherry yourself, come over and see me," Mr. Prentice went on. "I'm generally back from my chambers around and about six. Markham and I don't have many visitors."

Mr. Prentice suddenly seemed to Mrs. Dawson to be rather a pathetic figure. It was a description of himself that Mr.

Prentice wouldn't have recognized—but Mrs. Dawson's eyes became very bright.

"You are being very good to me," she said.

Mr. Speed, who had managed to focus Mr. Prentice at long last, put out his great fist and pointed a shaking finger at him.

"What the devil are you doing in here?" he asked.

"He's come to see you home," Mrs. Dawson informed him with confidence.

"I never saw him come in," Mr. Speed said suspiciously. Mr. Prentice opened the door and Lottie Spate rushed out, glad to escape from human society for a little.

"Are you coming, Mr. Speed?" Mr. Prentice asked him softly.

Mr. Speed drew himself up to the full extent of his enormous height and bulk.

"Of course I'm coming," he said. "I know when I'm not wanted." He looked at Mrs. Dawson. "But I'm not coming round again, Violette. Let's be quite clear on that."

"I'm glad you're clear about something, Jimmie," she answered him lightly.

"I suppose," he said as he pushed past her in the narrow hall, "you don't know where she's gone."

"I don't, and I don't care," Mrs. Dawson replied in a flat voice, "and I should advise you to adopt the same philosophy."

"Thanks," Mr. Speed said curtly and lurched through the door into the courtyard where Mr. Prentice was watching for him apprehensively.

If Mr. Prentice thought he was going to return to his own house he soon found out his mistake, for Mr. Speed's great hand closed upon his arm and he found himself walking somewhat irregularly in the opposite direction.

"I must get to bed," he protested, but Mr. Speed paid no attention to his words and, occasionally leaning on him and occasionally thrusting him forward, propelled him to the door of Number 3, where they arrived after having avoided the ash tree in the centre of the courtyard only with the greatest of difficulty. They also took considerably longer than necessary to get into the house because Mr. Speed insisted on putting

the key into the lock himself, while Mr. Prentice tried to keep
his eyes both on his dog and on Mr. Speed's unsteady hand.
As Mr. Speed found the key's billet and surprised himself so
much that he entered his own house much in the same way
as he had previously entered Mrs. Dawson's, Mr. Prentice
wondered vaguely whether Lottie Spate had any opinion
upon her master's novel way of spending his evenings, which
were in great contrast to the old sedate times in and about
King's Bench Walk. An idea that now that Mr. Speed had
let go his arm he might make his escape had hardly entered
Mr. Prentice's head when he had to forgo it because Lottie
Spate, unable to resist the open door, had followed Mr.
Speed's unsteady feet.

"Is that spaniel a dog or a bitch?" Mr. Speed asked him
when they were all three looking at each other in Mr. Speed's
sitting-room.

"A bitch," Mr. Prentice replied.

"I thought so," Mr. Speed announced with solemnity.
"And I don't like women any more. Not at all." Contrary
to Mr. Prentice's expectation and much to his relief Mr.
Speed did not offer him a drink, but flinging himself down in
his armchair contemplated the chromium-plated clock let
into the wall with malignant eyes. "She's no business to talk
to me like that. No business at all. What do you think, Mr.
Dentist?"

"Prentice," Mr. Prentice repeated his name mildly. "I
don't know anything about it," he added hastily.

"There was a time when Violette would have been only
too pleased to get her hands on me," Mr. Speed said sombrely.
"When that foreign Adonis left her flatter and softer than any
stinking piece of plaice. I told her it would happen, but
women never listen. She's got points, too, has Violette."

"She's a very nice woman," Mr. Prentice said.

Mr. Speed raised his taurine head and gave Mr. Prentice
a prolonged and incredulous look from his bloodshot but
lively eyes. Still staring at him he wiped the sweat which had
gathered in gouts upon his forehead away with the back of his
sleeve and, at length, found his voice.

"Sit down," he said explosively. "You'll only look half

the fool that you do standing up." While Mr. Prentice subsided weakly into a chair Mr. Speed threw back his head and laughed. It was not a laugh charged with anything unpleasant; it was a friendly, almost boyish laugh. "A nice woman," he repeated, rolling the words round in his mouth to enjoy their full flavour. Then he stopped laughing abruptly and regarded Mr. Prentice with great earnestness. "She's a whore," he announced solemnly. "And to think there was a time when I might have married her."

"She might not have married you," Mr. Prentice put in.

"Don't be more absurd than you look," Mr. Speed put in. "Anyway it's of no importance—none at all." Mr. Speed fell into a gloomy silence.

"I gather Lady Iris had something to do with your—er—escape," Mr. Prentice spoke tentatively, wondering if her name would cause the same obstinate silence as it had done previously. But this time Mr. Speed showed no sign of any resentment except against Iris herself.

"It's a pity I ever saw her," he muttered. "Life'd have been a great deal different. I never thought you could get a woman in your blood. Drink! Yes. Diabetes! Yes. But not a woman."

"She was very beautiful?" Mr. Prentice asked, and he kept his voice so low that he wasn't quite certain whether Mr. Speed had heard him or not.

"Beautiful?" Mr. Speed repeated the word at last. "I wouldn't know. What is beauty?" He looked at Mr. Prentice and laughed again. "But it's not much good asking you. You don't even know the meaning of the word nice." His expression suddenly became solemn again as if some unseen hand had wiped away the laughter with a flick of a wet towel. "I was standing by the window in here exactly a year ago to-day when I saw her for the first time, and exactly two minutes later I was speaking to her, asking her if I could help her move in." He smiled sourly to himself. "She had, of course, already moved in. From that moment to this I haven't had a moment's peace."

"And Mrs. Dawson? Violette?" Mr. Prentice asked. Mr Speed shrugged his shoulders.

D

"One man or another, it makes no difference to that type of woman. But Iris—I thought at first it was a trick," he went on, "but afterwards I knew it wasn't. She always appeared to see beyond the immediate present, to be looking into a world of her own, so to speak. She was withdrawn and remote. It wasn't anything tangible, but it drew one. A mirage does it and when you get there there's Fanny Adams."

"And when you got there?" Mr. Prentice prompted him.

"I never got there," Mr. Speed answered him harshly. "And I don't suppose I ever shall now. But it wasn't for want of trying; I can assure you of that. I'm not one of your mingy little men who flutter around a woman, afraid of this and terrified of that." He put out his great chest a little. "I go for anything hell for leather. I take chances on everything. I don't think I was let loose on this earth to make the place happier for other people: I am here to try and make it liveable for myself. Current account, that's what I live on, and it's apt to be a big one." He paused. "Iris, I suppose, is just one of those things," he went on. "She came like thistledown and I jumped about like an elephant after her, and like thistledown she went."

"Where?"

Mr. Speed rose to his feet and once more wiped the sweat away from his forehead.

"If I knew where," he answered him deliberately, "I shouldn't be punishing the bottle, fogging my judgment and pulling my punches. I've missed a lot of opportunities lately because I can't concentrate or I lose my nerve or it's a bit of both. Damned silly effort with Violette to-night. I know there's some fellow keeping her and I don't want her anyway. Just plain stupid, that's what it was." He went over to the cabinet and poured himself out a drink. "But I've got to snap out of this," he went on, "otherwise it'll be too bad. You don't know where she is, I suppose?" He shot the question at Mr. Prentice with such aplomb and determination that the latter was almost startled into incoherency.

"N—no—I rather wanted to know myself," Mr. Prentice stammered.

"What for?"

"I d—don't really know," Mr. Prentice stammered.

"I think you're half witted." Mr. Speed gave his opinion in a judicial, unprejudiced fashion. "I've written to her," he went on more to himself than to Mr. Prentice, "once, sometimes twice a day, and there's no damned answer. What's a man to do? I can't trail the whole of the British Isles for her and she may be abroad. I wish to God I'd never seen her!"

"Mr. Fawcett doesn't know where she is either," Mr. Prentice said.

He didn't know quite why Mr. Fawcett's existence should have occurred to him at that moment, but Mr. Speed didn't seem to think the interpolation odd. All he did was to throw back his head and laugh again, this time with more vigour and abandon.

"Fawcett! She turned him upside down as well," he said with relish. "He barged in here this morning at about half-past eleven when all gentlemen should be in bed, unless they're going racing, and gave me a short lecture on the evils of drink. He had to make it short because I threw him out. All the same, he wasn't so concerned with my recent habit as with Iris." He paused and, looking at Mr. Prentice a little owlishly, finished, "he was always popping round on the pretence of saving her soul." Mr. Speed waggled his finger at Mr. Prentice. "But I know better. I told him once that there were plenty of bad souls in ugly bodies and those were the ones in need of salvation." He paused and poured the remainder of his drink down his throat. "I knew Fawcett didn't know where she was; that's what he came round to find out. Just before I shot him out I told him she'd gone to the Tregenna Castle hotel at St. Ives."

"Whatever for?" Mr. Prentice asked.

"It was as far away as I could think of at eleven-thirty in the morning in my pyjamas," Mr. Speed said. "I've thought of other hotels much further away since; and when he comes back maybe I'll think one of them up for him."

"You mean he's actually gone?" Mr. Prentice said.

"I don't know whether he's actually gone, but he'll

certainly go unless you interfere," Mr. Speed replied. "And if you do I'll break your neck," he added urbanely.

"I've no desire to have my neck broken," Mr. Prentice answered very quickly.

"That's all right then."

Mr. Prentice looked at the clock and, seeing that the time was close upon midnight, walked with hurried steps towards the door, snapping his fingers at Lottie Spate to follow him. Mr. Speed made no attempt to detain him any further: indeed, he appeared to have lost all interest in him and gazed at the curtained window immediately in front of him—a solitary, somewhat grotesque figure—bewildered and a little sorry for himself, a combination of feelings that had never before overwhelmed him.

As he was going out Mr. Prentice turned to bid him good-night in neighbourly fashion, but as he was about to do so another odd circumstance jogged his memory and became suddenly a matter of some significance.

"By the way, I gather from Mrs. Cumming that her husband has gone away," he said.

Mr. Speed pulled his mind together with an obvious effort; but when, after a minute, he had succeeded in understanding exactly what Mr. Prentice had said he showed every sign of interest.

"Cumming gone away? You mean without his wife?" he said. "Where?"

Mr. Speed put the question with great emphasis and it seemed to Mr. Prentice that he attached a certain importance to what was, on the face of it, a very insignificant event.

"I don't know where," Mr. Prentice replied. "As a matter of fact, I don't think his wife knows where he is," he went on in worried tones. "He did say to me a couple of nights ago that his wife and he might be going away, but obviously he never intended to take her."

"If he's after what I think he is, he'd hardly take Joyce," Mr. Speed said, throwing his head back and giving one of his explosive laughs. Then he became apprehensive. "He can't know any more than I do," he muttered to himself. "He's guessing; he must be."

"Guessing at what?" Mr. Prentice asked.

"Where Iris might be, of course," Mr. Speed answered impatiently and, picking up his empty glass, prepared to refill it. As he did so he looked at Mr. Prentice over the top of the cabinet. "If you're going, go; and if you're staying, stay, but for God's sake don't hang about," he told him.

Mr. Prentice made a hasty departure and scuttled across to his own house where, on opening the door, he found every light in the place on. For a moment he stood still in wonderment, then he made a tour of the lower part of the house turning the lights out as he left the rooms, and was about to mount the stairs when he heard a key turn in the lock and Markham came in.

"Where have you been?" Mr. Prentice asked him.

"I thought I'd take a walk," Markham answered.

Mr. Prentice regarded him with curiosity. Taking walks about midnight was not a practice of Markham's. Indeed, he had never known him to do such a thing before. In addition there was an expression on his face that was a mixture of wariness and fearfulness.

"You're afraid of something," Mr. Prentice challenged him. "I thought you were last night. What is it?"

Markham's thin lips set in a very firm line and an obstinate look came into his eyes.

"Me! Afraid!" he exclaimed at length. "What on earth should I be afraid of?"

His show of indignation, however, was not very convincing to Mr. Prentice.

"Why did you leave all the lights on?" he asked.

"Did I?" Markham replied. "I'm sorry."

He went past Mr. Prentice and up the stairs to bed leaving his master looking after him with a puzzled expression on his chubby face, and a certain uneasiness in his stomach. It was absurd for Markham to say that he was not afraid. He had left the house for no stroll. In fact, Mr. Prentice very much doubted whether he had walked beyond the gateway. Mr. Prentice suspected that he had stood awaiting his return and immediately he had seen him leave Number 3 had come in on his heels. Markham, who was a matter of fact and ordinary fellow, had turned on all the lights to find something or someone and, not finding what he had sought, had become afraid and walked out of the closed box into the open space where he had the man in the street for company and a long view for his eyes.

Mr. Prentice reconstructed Markham's behaviour thus, but he told himself that he would not cast that curious glance round his own room which he had bestowed on it the previous evening. He had been somewhat taken aback then, as he was now; but there was nothing wrong with the house, he was certain of that, and nothing about it that was not straightforward. Suiting his actions to his thoughts he went to his room, treading the carpet with heavy footsteps lest Markham should fear any stealthy intruder and, shutting his door with a certain force, put himself to bed in the same methodical way that had hitherto been his custom. But he did not put himself to sleep for a long time and more than once he caught himself listening for something; he did not know what. But though he heard many sounds, the wind flirting with the curtain, the low rumble of an occasional vehicle, the creak of wood expanding or contracting—Mr. Prentice never knew exactly what wood did in the night—and other tiny movements, he didn't hear what he didn't expect to hear and, at length, his heart was stilled, his pulse quietened and his senses numbed so that he fell asleep to dream of a woman in a white robe of heavy silk through which at regular intervals ran thin threads of the finest gold; a woman whose small feet winked at him through her sandals and in one of whose hands a staff was held aloft. In his dream it seemed imperative to him that he should catch the woman, but every time he made a great effort to do so he found himself toiling after her in vain. He only saw her straight back, her dark braided hair and heard her low laugh as she fled in front of him down the aisles of time.

In the morning Markham found him still asleep when he called him, a very unusual occurrence, and when he had dressed and come downstairs to breakfast, Markham surprised him by presenting him not only with the morning papers, but also with a small parcel. Mr. Prentice regarded it with high curiosity.

"I found it when I took in the milk," Markham said. "As it was addressed to you I thought it must be for you. The handwriting is awful and there is no esquire."

Mr. Prentice looked at the writing with great care.

"I don't think I ought to be called esquire," he said. "In fact, I am sure I should not. An esquire is a gentleman entitled to bear arms. In any case there are no initials and for some reason or other one never sees a surname without initials followed by esquire. I should say this is a child's handwriting."

"If you'd open it you'd find out," Markham said.

Mr. Prentice sighed at his logical attitude and was about to launch into a disquisition on the sweets of surprise when Markham's air of utter misery made him change his mind, and he pulled the loosely tied string from the wrapping. It was a thin package, rectangular in shape, and hard. Mr. Prentice would have liked to have wasted a considerable time guessing its nature, but he knew that Markham would never leave him until he knew what the brown paper concealed.

"I expect it's a sample," Markham said.

"As the package has no stamps on it," Mr. Prentice replied, "I should think it's most unlikely."

Slowly he drew it from the paper and, smiling at him from an ebony frame, was the picture of a woman. Behind her were draped heavy curtains as full of folds as pieces of corrugated iron; in the foreground she leaned with one arm upon what Mr. Prentice took to be a sundial. Her hands and forearms were encased in long white gloves, and her luxurious hair swept wide and tousled about her head on which was perched a hat of monstrous size, stuffed with ostrich feathers. A long white dress fell to her ankles where her small feet in white satin slippers peeped out. Her compact, pretty face with its tiny impudent nose, was wreathed in one large smile and her laughing mouth disclosed two rows of brilliant teeth.

Markham, looking over his master's shoulders, became the more disappointed as he studied the whole picture.

"Who's sent you a thing like that?" he asked as he picked up the paper and searched for a card or some message; but

Mr. Prentice, holding the picture in both his hands and continuing to look at it, his brown eyes alight with admiration, made no reply.

"Who is it, anyway?" Markham tried again.

"It's a funny thing," Mr. Prentice murmured, "I don't remember this picture at all. Perhaps it's a private one."

"Looks like an actress to me," Markham said, his voice laden with disgust.

Mr. Prentice put the picture down by his side with a sigh.

"That, my dear Markham," he announced as he picked up his knife and fork, "is the great, the incomparable, the never-to-be-forgotten, the one and only Lottie Spate."

"Well, I don't think much of her," Markham replied with no sign of surprise. "Anyway she's dead, isn't she?"

Mr. Prentice nodded his head.

"A long time," he said. "So you don't think much of her, don't you? Well, I don't suppose she'd have thought much of us if it comes to that. But when I was young I didn't dream of a woman in white samite; I dreamed of Lottie Spate. And someone has been kind enough to return my youth to me, or rather to recall it. One forgets too easily the pleasures that are past. But this is very opportune. Perhaps it was meant to be."

"Who's given it to you?" Markham tried again.

Mr. Prentice went on eating his bacon and sipping his tea in silence for a moment or two.

"A nice woman," he replied at length. "I hope she'll come round here some evening." He looked up. "And if by any chance her child should take it into her head to look us up and I'm not here, I hope that you'll try and interest her in something."

"Do you mean that child across the way?" Markham asked.

"I do. Paula and her mother, Mrs. Dawson," Mr. Prentice replied.

"I thought we weren't going to have anything to do with the neighbours," Markham said.

Mr. Prentice picked up the photograph again and scrutinized it.

"Why, of course, what a fool I am!" he exclaimed. "No wonder she was so interested in Lottie Spate."

"I don't know what you're talking about," Markham said, "but if you don't get a move on you'll be late at chambers."

Mr. Prentice put down the photograph again and taking up the morning papers rose to his feet.

"Buy a nice bunch of flowers for me," he said, "and give them to Paula with my compliments. You may also say that I shall be delighted to see either her or her mother over here any time."

"What kind of flowers?"

"What sort of flowers does one give to a little girl of four or five?" Mr. Prentice asked himself. "Roses, I should think. Yes, red roses."

"I shall want some money," Markham said stubbornly, hoping that the matter of money might turn aside his master's whim. But Mr. Prentice only took out his notecase and, throwing a pound note upon the table, gathered up the picture.

"You and I," he said, "must go into the economics of our new life sometime soon. We must find some way to cut down expenses."

He turned into the study where he put the picture in the middle of the mantelpiece. Markham followed him, holding his hat and umbrella.

"Let's sell the house and live somewhere cheaper," he suggested.

Mr. Prentice swung round from his contemplation of the photograph in its new position.

"You'd like to leave here?" he said.

"I certainly should," Markham answered, and there was a fervid note in his voice which overbore its usual mournfulness.

"Now why?" Mr. Prentice asked softly. "I should like to know that."

Markham hesitated and then handed him his hat and umbrella more, it seemed to Mr. Prentice, from a desire to be doing something than because he thought it was necessary that at that precise moment he should get rid of him.

"If it's too expensive," Markham muttered, "surely it's better——" he drifted away into silence and, when he thought Mr. Prentice was about to return to the attack, abruptly left the room. Mr. Prentice looked after him thoughtfully, then picking up his brief case and thrusting the morning papers and a couple of briefs into it, blew a kiss towards the picture and left the house with a jauntier gait than usual.

"Expense," he thought to himself. "I am starting 'to die beyond my means' and yet I ought to be able to afford to live in that house. It's the taxation. I can't understand why the young people don't clear out—perhaps they do." He shrugged his shoulders and clambering onto his bus opened his newspaper.

The gaiety induced by the photograph was not of long duration and by the time Mr. Prentice had reached his chambers the call from the past sounded very faintly in his ears. There was no doubt about the matter at all; he would have to go into a committee of ways and means with Markham and discover in what way expenditure could be reduced. He had always, hitherto, lived within his income and failure to do this sent unpleasant shivers down his spine, even though he comforted himself with the thought that many of his bills lately had been of a non-recurring nature. The cost of removal and of the interior decoration, for instance, were such; and he told himself that if he could lay his hands on a sum of money which was outside his usual income, he could put himself straight again and could probably keep himself on the right side. The margin was a slender one, but it was there.

He looked hopefully at the clerk of the chambers as he entered his office, but the clerk's greeting and demeanour told him that he would find nothing unexpected and, indeed, he didn't. There were a couple of new briefs, what he called "chicken feed", lying on his desk, but these gave no promise of developing into a really expensive legal battle. They were part and parcel of what had been his practice for many years; the sum of them all made a comfortable income for him, but it did not allow him any margin for contingencies, not even for a long vacation. He had always worked through nearly all of that, picking up scraps that his more successful colleagues could afford to ignore while they went away for a couple of months of amusement and refused to have their holidays interrupted under three figures.

Sitting down at the desk he tumbled out the briefs from his case and, ringing the bell, gave them to the clerk. Then he picked up the two new ones.

"Mr. Trevor's coming to see you at half-past ten; he wants the Company one stood over, he's not ready. He'd be glad if you'd settle the form of writ in the other."

"What's it about? Any idea?" he asked.

"He didn't say. He only said it was a small matter."

Mr. Prentice pushed the papers away from him and sighed.

"I wish you could manage to lay your hands on something really worth while," he said.

"There isn't a great deal doing anywhere, Mr. Prentice," the clerk answered hastily. "Things are very slack all round."

"Oh, I know you do your best," Mr. Prentice replied with equal haste. "I didn't mean that. Though it's true my practice doesn't diminish, it's also true that it doesn't grow. If there are no neap tides, there are also no spring ones. The high water mark is stationary like that on a dirty boy's neck. I could do with a spring tide just about now."

The clerk looked a little worried.

"Something'll probably turn up, Mr. Prentice," he said more cheerfully. "I saw Gatlen yesterday and he told me they had a nice fat chancery action coming on shortly, but then," he looked troubled again, "they nearly always go to Mr. Hepburn."

As Mr. Prentice didn't answer him the clerk turned away with the completed conveyance in his hand, but he didn't look nearly so cheerful as he had when Mr. Prentice arrived. He had noticed a change in Mr. Prentice lately and dated it from the time Mr. Prentice had had to give up his flat on the other side of the street. Before that Mr. Prentice had never seemed to worry about anything and was perfectly content with the volume and content of his work; but during the last day or two his happy disposition had been overcast. The clerk did not want anything or anyone to upset any of his gentlemen.

It was not until Mr. Prentice returned in the evening that he found himself once again thinking of Iris. Throughout the day, sometimes only with a great effort of will, he had put all thoughts of her aside, but once he entered the courtyard again and his eyes fell upon the marigolds, he found himself turning over and over in his mind his previous night's conversations with his opposite neighbours. He kept on telling himself that it was no business of his, but the more he wished he had never allowed himself to be curious, the more his curiosity spurred him. She had known all the inmates of the court whom he had himself met, known them apparently well, and yet had vanished leaving none of them with any idea where she had gone. Fawcett had thundered, Speed had taken to drink, Cumming had dithered, the two women had stood aloof, cold and hostile, and the little girl had cried. Cumming had gone after her, that was what Speed had implied; Fawcett had been sent after her on a fruitless errand while Speed remained where he was. Mr. Prentice had no doubt that Speed, not knowing what to do, had wisely decided to do nothing except watch and wait for some definite news, or her return. Mr. Prentice had also no doubt now that the interest of the dwellers in the court in himself was not inspired by his person, but arose from a desire to discover his connections, if any, with the late tenant. In probing for those they had one by one whetted his own appetite until he found himself caught up in the gossamer threads of a mystery from which, like any fly, he tried in vain to break loose.

So far Mr. Prentice had dealt with the facts, scanty enough, which he had been able to piece together; he was able also to make a few deductions from those facts which sprang from the remarks which one or the other of the people who were interested had dropped. If the whole business had rested there Mr. Prentice felt that he would not have been so troubled; but there was an undercurrent of something he did not understand. There was a knocking on the doors of his consciousness, faint at first, but insistent and now louder, whose urgency appeared to increase as the hours trailed past. It was true that the violence of it receded during the day, but it was also true that it was with him like his shadow and it was that, and not the problem itself, if there was one, that was giving him increasing concern. Concern was too slight a description, he felt, of what he was beginning to feel; that had been succeeded by apprehension, and apprehension was rapidly being submerged by an emotion very much stronger.

"What is the most powerful emotion in the world?" He put the question to Lottie Spate and the dog wagged her tail. "No, you are wrong, my dear," Mr. Prentice muttered in the same breath. "It is not love; that is the popular notion; it suits the romanticists. And I suppose as one myself it should be sufficient answer for me. But I am in grave doubt about it. I am inclined, I won't put it higher yet, but I am inclined to think the answer is fear. That is the greatest emotion in the world; it is more powerful, more puissant than hate. It is that, and not love, which makes the world go round. It spins the globe at all times and, if it is an aphorism that every second the fruits of love are being gathered, it is also true that there is not a second in all eternity that man is not afraid of someone or something. And if you sub-divide fear, so to speak, the strongest of all the sub-divisions is the fear of the unknown. When you can't put your finger on the cause and at the same time feel the effect. A sudden oppression in the air and yet no sign of a storm; a rustling in the leaves and yet no wind; a sense of company and yet no person. Animals are, I believe, supposed to be proner to this sort of terror than human beings, but there may be some confusion of thought here. Animals don't, I believe, fear the unknown so much as register their fear of the known before human beings, because their senses being keener they become aware more quickly." He looked at Lottie Spate shrewdly. "At any rate you don't seem to be troubled," he concluded, "but I am—very. And so, I rather think, is Markham. What manner of woman is this Iris?" he asked, and sat moodily in his chair searching for an answer until Markham came in. Mr. Prentice gave him a sharp look, but Markham's face appeared to be as impassive and miserable as usual.

"I took the flowers over," he said.

Mr. Prentice gave the picture on the mantelpiece a fleeting glance.

"Good," he answered. "I hope you made a nice little speech."

"I said what you told me to say about the little girl or her mother coming over here some time if they felt like it."

"And I suppose looked as if you hoped they'd never feel like it," Mr. Prentice put in.

Markham looked a little shocked.

"No, I didn't," he replied. "But I didn't bargain for the offer being accepted on the nail, as it were." Mr. Prentice raised his eyebrows in surprise. "There was a young fair fellow there whom Mrs. Dawson called Toddy—or at any rate that's what it sounded like, and the moment I'd given the invitation and flowers to Paula he said, 'Could you manage to-day. Could you give Paula lunch?' I was so taken aback I said, 'Yes, I suppose so,' before I'd given myself time to think. Mrs. Dawson was a bit embarrassed, but naturally Paula came over here."

Mr. Prentice looked at Markham and a smile, full of sympathy for his predicament, wreathed his face. Nothing, he felt sure, could have been more irksome for Markham than to have found himself saddled with a child for a meal, and probably for most of the afternoon. It was really very inconsiderate of Toddy.

"I'm sorry to have let you in for that," he said. "I didn't mean Paula to come over here unless I was in myself. I know your views on children."

"I didn't mind so much," Markham admitted. "As a matter of fact I was quite glad of her company."

"You were what!" Mr. Prentice exclaimed.

"I was quite pleased to see her," Markham repeated stubbornly, "and in a way she was no trouble at all. She's very self-possessed for a little girl of her age, but she's a little odd," he added, after hesitating a moment as if he was having a certain amount of difficulty in picking out the right word.

The smile left Mr. Prentice's face and he gave his servant a sharp look which made Markham shift his eyes hurriedly as he tried to avoid it.

"Odd!" Mr. Prentice exclaimed. "What's odd about her?"

Markham frowned and scratched the back of his head in perplexity.

"She seems an ordinary child to me—if rather a pretty one," Mr. Prentice went on, pressing him for an answer. "I don't see anything particularly unusual about her."

"Not in her manner or anything, no," Markham replied at last in a voice full of doubt. "But she told me some very—well, unusual stories," he blurted out.

"Told you stories?" Mr. Prentice repeated blankly.

Markham shuffled a little uncomfortably and his customary dejected expression seemed to Mr. Prentice to be further accentuated.

"Well, she asked me to tell her some," he explained, "but it's a very long time since I heard a fairy story, let alone read one. I had a shot at Cinderella but she knew that, and then I tried Aladdin but she knew that. So in the end I asked her to tell me some and she did and they were very unusual. In fact I'd never heard anything like them. Most peculiar and very queer names."

"Such as?" Mr. Prentice asked.

"Well, here is one I remember. Apparently there was a King and Queen," Markham began hazily, "and there was a gentleman whose name I couldn't quite get hold of, but it sounded like Lion. He was bound to a wheel in the end——"

"Bound to a wheel? Lion?" Mr. Prentice repeated. "It wasn't Ixion, I suppose," he suggested tentatively after a moment.

Markham looked at him with some respect.

"That's the fellow," he acknowledged and seeming to gain confidence continued the story apace. "Paula said he was a wicked man who killed his wife's father by throwing him into a flaming pit, and when the King sent for him he fell in love with the Queen: so the King made a likeness of the Queen out of clouds. Ixion apparently mistook the ghost for the Queen and went about the place saying that the Queen herself was in love with him. This so upset the King that he had him tied to a wheel where he goes on turning round and round. Very unpleasant, I should say."

Mr. Prentice put his fingers together and looked at the photograph of Lottie Spate through the pent he had made.

"The story is not quite as bald as all that," he said. "Where did Paula get it from?" he asked.

Markham looked a little uncomfortable.

"She told me Lady Iris used to tell her stories," he said.

Mr. Prentice brought his hands away from his face sharply and, sitting up, gave Markham his whole attention.

"Lady Iris," he repeated softly. "And what else did she tell you about her?"

"Nothing, except that her mother didn't like her and she did. But she didn't think she was very happy," Markham answered. "I don't understand her telling the child stories like that," he went on.

"Yes, I expect Aladdin or Cinderella seem a little insipid," Mr. Prentice replied absent-mindedly. "She didn't know, by any chance, where Lady Iris had gone, I suppose?" he went on, looking at Markham keenly.

"No, I asked her," Markham replied.

"Now why did you do that?" Mr. Prentice asked him curiously. "What do you want to know for?"

Markham dropped his eyes before the sharp ones of Mr. Prentice.

"I'd just like to know," he muttered. Then he raised his eyes again and Mr. Prentice caught a gleam in them of something like defiance. "And so would someone else."

"Who?" Mr. Prentice asked mildly, expecting Markham to name himself, but he didn't do anything of the kind.

"Mr. Cumming," he said.

"Has he been here?" Mr. Prentice asked in astonished tones.

"He nearly pushed the bell into its socket for good and all at about half-past four this afternoon and when I opened the door, thinking the place was on fire or something, he pushed his way in and asked for you. I told him you were at your chambers and he muttered something about what a fool he was and, of course, you were."

"I suppose he meant, of course, I was at the Law Courts.

It sounds, the way you put it, as if he thought I was an idiot too," Mr. Prentice objected.

"Maybe he meant it that way," Markham replied. "He was in a terrible state. Didn't look as if he'd slept for nights and he was white and shivering."

"Did he tell you why he wanted me?" Mr. Prentice asked.

"No, but he asked me if I'd seen anything of Lady Iris while he'd been away."

"And you haven't, have you?" Mr. Prentice said.

Markham hesitated; it was only momentary, then his chin was thrust out.

"No," he replied decidedly.

"And where did Mr. Cumming go?" Mr. Prentice asked, after he had waited to see whether Markham was going to amplify his negative.

"He rushed straight across the courtyard and out of the gateway," Markham answered, walking slowly towards the door. When he reached it he turned round and gave Mr. Prentice a long and impassive look. "I don't like the way things are." It was a statement of fact, unvarnished and delivered without emotion. Then he turned on his heels and went quickly out. Mr. Prentice's good-natured face puckered and, getting quickly to his feet, he went towards the fireplace with no clear idea in his head why he had got up and why he had gone there.

"Neither do I," he muttered.

Finding himself face to face with the photograph of Lottie Spate he took it down and gazed at it. The sight of it carried him back to the uncomfortable and noisy gallery and to the days of what had been peace and what had seemed to him to be plenty. He was preparing to indulge himself in a bath made of sweet waters from the past when the door was opened and Markham appeared again.

"Mrs. Cumming would like a word with you, if it's convenient," Markham said as Mr. Prentice hastily put the photograph back.

"Of course, of course," he answered hurriedly. "Let her come in."

Joyce Cumming came in while he was still speaking and Mr. Prentice went at once to the corner cupboard.

"You've come to continue the sherry drinking," he said.

"Nothing I'd like better," she replied, but in spite of the languid gaiety in her voice Mr. Prentice detected, or thought he did, a note of bravado and, turning round to look at her, saw her body stiff and unyielding under her dress and her eyes, heavy but remorseless, not looking at him but at the photograph on the mantelpiece.

"Hullo, she's new!" she exclaimed, but without any enthusiasm. Then she went over to it while he pulled out the decanter and the glasses. "Fetching, I call her," she went on. "I love that period in British history when sundials lived in drawing-rooms."

"I believe—in fact I'm sure that's Mrs. Dawson's mother; there's a distinct resemblance," Mr. Prentice told her. "My first and only love," he went on rather proudly. "Though, of course, I have had other—what you might call—inclinations."

Joyce Cumming reached out for the glass which he had left on the table for her.

"Don't tell me Violette is your daughter!" she exclaimed. "That would be very cosy, wouldn't it?"

"Alas, no," Mr. Prentice replied. "Mine was 'the desire of the moth for the star, of the night for the morrow, the devotion to something afar from the sphere of our sorrow'."

"Touching," Joyce Cumming said, sipping her drink. "I imagined that at least you drank bubbly out of her slipper, which I should think is more than anyone would do out of Violette's."

Mr. Prentice looked at her thoughtfully and sighed.

"You are out of humour," he said. "I found Mrs. Dawson very nice; but I don't think she'd let me drink out of her slipper, even if I wanted to do so."

"I rather think you're a bit late on the scene," Joyce replied. "Not that I bear her any malice; but she is a bit obvious, you know."

"I suppose her hair is a bit startling," Mr. Prentice acknowledged.

"I've seen more startling heads than that," Joyce said. "I wasn't thinking of her appearance. I was thinking of an expensive motor car." She shrugged her shoulders. "However, it's no business of mine. But I shouldn't have thought all that sort of thing much good for the child."

"There is that, of course," Mr. Prentice murmured. "I suppose as you don't know her very well, you've no idea who——" he stopped abruptly.

"Who what?" Joyce asked him.

Mr. Prentice hesitated.

"I was wondering who a gentleman called Toddy is," he admitted a little shamefacedly.

Joyce Cumming was in the act of raising her drink to her mouth when Mr. Prentice made his admission, and she lowered it again quickly while her eyes, which before had been dark still pools, flashed with surprise.

"What on earth has she got to do with Toddy?" she asked.

Mr. Prentice looked still more uncomfortable.

"Nothing," he answered. "I only——"

"When did you get to know Mrs. Dawson so well?" Joyce pressed him.

"As a matter of fact we had a little chat last night," Mr. Prentice said.

"And Toddy was there?" Joyce asked him in a surprised voice.

"Yes, he was," Mr. Prentice admitted at length. "Only she forgot to introduce me."

Joyce Cumming laughed. Mr. Prentice thought it a very pleasant sound—like tumbling waters, for there was no malice in it, just enjoyment.

"Then I imagine she didn't want you to know who he was," she replied. "And that may mean——" She paused and then went on again, apparently at a tangent. "I must say, it's rather fun. They must have been very clever about it. Though I thought I caught a glimpse of him this morning. That motor car, too. I suppose I should have known, but then all expensive cars, except the Rolls, look the same to me."

She looked at the tubby form of Mr. Prentice and appeared for the first time to take him in as a whole. Mr. Prentice withstood her scrutiny, but not without a certain embarrassment.

"I think perhaps we'd better drop the subject," he said.

"Drop it? What for?" Joyce asked. "I owe Violette something for the way that child of hers keeps on screaming. Besides, it doesn't matter a hoot anyway. Toddy is the Honourable Edward Todhunter."

"Lady Iris's brother!" Mr. Prentice exclaimed.

Joyce Cumming nodded.

"Younger brother," she corrected him. "Which brings me to the object of my visit," she added inconsequently. "Have you seen my husband? He waltzed in and out of the courtyard this afternoon; I saw him myself. I had the proverbial light in the window, but he didn't see it." She sipped her sherry deliberately. "Or if he did, he ignored it. In short, like Miss Otis, he is unable to dine to-night, but unlike her sent no message of regret."

Mr. Prentice suddenly felt very sorry for her; she was putting a bold face on things, but it was plain to him that she was badly hurt, and probably for the first time in her life uncertain of herself though no one, without some knowledge of the circumstances, would have guessed it from the poise of her head and the straightness of her carriage.

"I believe he did call here," Mr. Prentice admitted awkwardly. "I wasn't in. Markham saw him."

"What did he want?" she asked and, when Mr. Prentice hesitated, waved his hesitancy away. "You needn't bother to tell me if you don't want to. He tried Fawcett and Speed as well; I saw him. But only Mrs. Fawcett was in and he bolted by way of you." She paused and gave another very deliberate look. "He wanted to try and find out where Iris is—and he must be in a pretty parlous condition to dash about here like a lunatic. He appears to have lost his head and that's somewhat of a pity because, between you and me, he can't afford to lose what little he has."

Mr. Prentice hastily grabbed the decanter and poured some more sherry into her glass, a little comforted to find that while his own hand was a trifle unsteady, hers was as firm as it was small.

"I think you are rather a pet," Joyce Cumming went on, as if there had been no interruption. "I mean it, you know. You're the kind of man who thinks all women are wonderful —especially the good-looking ones. I suppose no one seized you when you were young because they didn't want to disillusion you." She waved her hand towards the photograph. "That's just typical of you. But women aren't the dear, romantic creatures you think they are." Mr. Prentice caught an echo of Mrs. Dawson as she spoke. "As a matter of fact, I don't suppose they ever were, but they used to think it rather sweet to be thought so. Now they don't give a damn. There's nothing romantic about me; or Iris or Violette, if it comes to that. So you won't be sorry for me, will you?"

Mr. Prentice came slowly towards her, his glass of sherry in one hand, and put the other arm round her shoulder as she sat perched on the arm of his chair.

"No, my dear, of course not," he replied as he patted her shoulder and drew her a little closer to him. Joyce leaned forward and put her glass of sherry unsteadily on the table.

"Oh, damn you, damn you, damn you!" she exclaimed and started to cry, with her fair head tucked into his waistcoat, while Mr. Prentice looked like an owl at her curls.

After a while she threw her head back and, dabbing her eyes with the backs of her hands, wriggled away from his protecting arm and, standing up, smoothed out her skirt.

"I'm sorry," she said. "I didn't come here to cry on your shoulder." She picked up her glass again and looked at Mr. Prentice with a touch of her old defiance. "I think I shall go away as well," she went on.

"I shouldn't do that," Mr. Prentice replied. "I expect your husband will——"

"Norman," she interrupted him, "will do what Iris tells him to do." She shrugged her shoulders. "I suppose I was a fool; it can't be helped now."

Mr. Prentice tried not to appear too interested; he had an idea that Joyce Cumming was rarely in a confidential mood and that any sign of undue interest on his part might cause her to retreat behind her own defences again.

"It would be a tiresome world if no one made a mistake," he said.

Joyce Cumming looked at him with contemplative eyes as if she were measuring his worth in some invisible balance that she held.

"I'd have done better to let things be," she said at length. "I nearly did and then something snapped inside me, but I frightened her"—a slow smile played upon her lips and she nodded her head in agreement with her words—"Oh yes, I frightened her all right," she went on, "but I didn't think she'd disappear."

Mr. Prentice once more assumed his pose of holding up his glass of sherry to the light and gazing at it intently as if he had detected a foreign substance and wanted to capture it.

"What did you say to her?" he asked.

"Say!" she exclaimed. "I didn't say very much at all. I just walked in here one evening with Norman's revolver and told her if she didn't clear out I'd shoot her."

Mr. Prentice suddenly felt cold. He was very afraid of violence believing, or wishing to believe, that there was no question which could not be solved by clear thinking in spite of the second world war in his lifetime.

Joyce Cumming gave him an oblique, queer smile.

"That doesn't fit in with your feminine theories, does it?" she quizzed him. "Women are expected to be afraid of revolvers; let alone threaten to use them. But Iris sold up her house and went; and that was what I thought I wanted. It seems now that her departure has caused more trouble than her arrival did." She finished her sherry. "Anyway all this has got nothing to do with you. I'm sorry if I bored you with it all."

Mr. Prentice decided to come out into the open.

"On the contrary, I am most interested," he replied. "But I must confess myself a little baffled. Mr. Speed seems to have taken her departure equally badly, and so does Mr. Fawcett. Where do they come in?"

Joyce Cumming looked at him a little grimly.

"They don't, so far as I know," she answered. "Jimmie

Speed was first on the scene," she admitted. "I used to find it rather amusing; but Iris didn't like him very much really. Then I found that Norman had ceased to laugh at Jimmie Speed and was beginning to be angry with him. Fawcett appeared last of all; he scented sin. Or at least that's what his excuse was. So the whole place was turned upside down and, in the middle of it all, walked Iris, aloof and in some respects a little lovely—I'll admit that." She tossed her head back. "So now you know the whole story; and she went as she came, like the wind, leaving behind her a riot of unrest. When I go I'm afraid no one will pay any attention."

"But you mustn't go," Mr. Prentice said, a note of alarm in his voice. "That wouldn't do at all."

"If Norman doesn't return soon and put my wedding ring back on my finger I certainly shall," she answered defiantly. "When I threw it out of the window I meant it; but you brought it back. The next time I throw it away I'll take good care no one brings it back."

"I hardly think, you know," Mr. Prentice began in a conciliatory manner, "that if Lady Iris had wanted to detach your husband she would have gone away without leaving any clue to her whereabouts."

"Don't you? Well, that depends on how afraid one is of being shot, I expect," Joyce Cumming replied contemptuously.

"You still have the revolver?" Mr. Prentice asked. She nodded to him.

"Oh yes," she admitted, "and I've got it in a safe place where Norman can't get hold of it. You can't reason with women over some things, you know, and there's always a danger that men won't reason with themselves." She smiled at him again. "You look frightened; you needn't be. I shan't use it now and, if Norman finds her and she wants him, he'd better go. There's no sense in three people being unhappy instead of one." As she moved towards the door, Mr. Prentice followed in her wake.

"She must have some extraordinary qualities so to attract men," he said in a low, meditative voice as if answering an unspoken question he had put to himself.

"Extraordinary? I don't think so," Joyce Cumming replied coolly. "After all, I am not unattractive myself and I could upset as many men quite easily if I wanted to."

But though Mr. Prentice didn't say so he was not satisfied with her answer. The truth was not so bald as that he was certain; and there was no evidence so far that Lady Iris had wanted to upset anyone. Yet, in some fashion she was even upsetting him and he had never known her.

"You must come and dine with us if Norman returns," she said, recovering her artificiality. "I'll make my mayonnaise sauce with liquid paraffin—it's very good for you. And if he doesn't you must come just the same and, if you won't do my divorce yourself, you can advise me of someone nice like yourself. I don't fancy airing my failures in public much." She didn't wait for him to show her out but went quickly and Mr. Prentice, perturbed and teetering on his feet, found himself alone before he was really certain that she had gone.

He knew now why Joyce, on her first entrance into his study, had hesitated and appeared unwilling to go forward into the room. He knew now why her husband had stared at all his furniture; it was not the room as it was, but as it had been, that he was remembering. Mr. Prentice thought he saw into the young man's mind as he had looked about him. He had been trying to recapture some little touch which should remind him of the former tenant, but the character of the room had been so altered that there was nothing left to recall her. She had vanished and the place was swept clear of her personality. He thought again about the revolver and shivered because he had a feeling that at the time Joyce had meant every word she said, but yet he could not bring himself to believe that the threat alone had been responsible for Lady Iris's disappearance. He was still wrapped up in his own surmises when Markham came in to tell him dinner was ready.

"Mr. Cumming come back yet?" he asked.

Mr. Prentice looked at him in surprise.

"I didn't know you knew he was away," he said.

"Must be," Markham replied. "Things are quiet—too

quiet," he added. "That queer chap from Number 5 has gone away too. Seems we'll have the place to ourselves soon."

"You mean Mr. Fawcett?" Mr. Prentice asked and, recalling what Jimmie Speed had told him he'd done, was not very surprised at the news. Markham nodded his assent.

"Paula and Mrs. Dawson are going away for the week-end to-night also," Markham went on. "Paula told me. They're going away to the seaside with that gentleman called Toddy, whoever he may be." Mr. Prentice just grunted. "That leaves us Mrs. Cumming, the dipso and a funny old female, Mrs. Fawcett I expect; and whoever lives in Number 2, but as he never appears he hardly counts."

Mr. Prentice became suddenly a little irritated.

"What does it matter?" he asked. "You never wanted any neighbours. Well, you won't have any."

"Will you be going up to the Courts to-morrow?" Markham asked.

"Not for long. It's Saturday. Why?" Mr. Prentice sounded still irritated.

"I wondered if you'd taken it into your head to go away as well," Markham said.

"Why should I? Supposing I have?" Mr. Prentice suddenly changed direction and watched Markham's face. He was rewarded with a quick look of apprehension.

"Have you?" he asked urgently.

"As a matter of fact, no," Mr. Prentice answered. Markham's sigh of relief was audible but he said no more.

Mr. Prentice was sorry to hear that Violette Dawson had gone away; he had wanted to have a long talk to her about her mother, to rake over the ashes of the past and to satisfy such youthful curiosity that remained to him. Did she, in fact, have red hair? This still seemed to Mr. Prentice to be a matter of paramount importance; it coloured all his dreams of her. At any rate her mother was the subject, he told himself, that he wanted to discuss with her; in reality while he toyed with the notion he found himself thinking more about the brother of Iris than anyone else. The impression which remained on his mind from their short and somewhat peculiar meeting was of a fair, thin young man with a pleasant, frank and open countenance who certainly had not appeared to be worried about anything or anyone, once he had made sure that no burglar was lurking in the house. Surely he must know where his sister was.

Markham interrupted his conjectures by coming in to his study to put the clean glasses back into the corner cupboard, but as he never replaced such things until the morning, Mr. Prentice viewed him over the top of his cigarette with a certain curiosity, and waited to hear what he was going to say when he had got rid of them.

"Thought you'd like to know that the dipso's gone too." Markham spoke with his back to Mr. Prentice as he shut the door of the cupboard with meticulous care.

"I take it you're referring to Mr. Speed," Mr. Prentice said.

"If that's his name," Markham replied. "Saw him go out with a bag while I was clearing away in the dining-room."

Mr. Prentice sat up in his chair and looked him over very keenly.

"What, exactly, are you afraid of?" he asked.

"Afraid!" Markham repeated in belligerent tones. "I'm not afraid of anything," he added in a less confident voice; but when he spoke he gave his master the impression that he was not so much listening to the question and answer of their own conversation, but that his ears were cocked to hear something or someone else. Mr. Prentice made a gesture towards the dining-room and the hall where, through the open study door, he could see all the lights blazing.

"I said we'd have to go into committee of ways and means sometime," he said. "You are getting very careless with the lights."

"I'll put them out," Markham muttered.

"But you'd rather not," Mr. Prentice said softly. "Why not, Markham?"

Markham looked very uncomfortable, but he stood his ground and, after a moment, raised his eyes to meet those of Mr. Prentice.

"I've never liked the house from the moment we came into it," he replied.

"But what's wrong with it?" Mr. Prentice asked.

Markham shook his head.

"I don't believe in putting thoughts into people's heads," he replied. "You sit about and see what's in front of your nose, but there's a heap of things in front of your nose that you don't see."

"Air, for instance," Mr. Prentice suggested. "Or shall I call it atmosphere?"

"And some people hear things that others don't," Markham said.

"Or think they hear them," Mr. Prentice replied severely. "What have you heard that I haven't?" he asked in more conciliatory tones.

Markham hesitated a little, then he put his head up as a man does who is determined to take his chance.

"I thought I heard a woman crying," he replied, "but if you didn't hear her, perhaps I was wrong."

Mr. Prentice stubbed his cigarette out in the ash tray very deliberately and kept his eyes to himself; but in spite of his apparent inattention he was listening very hard.

"It was probably Paula," he said, "or Mrs. Cumming next door; the walls are not as thick as they used to be; we live in a shoddy age."

"Perhaps," Markham answered without any conviction in his voice and moved away slowly to the hall.

When the door shut behind him Mr. Prentice suddenly felt very tired, as if he had taken part in some tremendous mental exercise, and the problem had put his mind through a mangle leaving it limp, dank and lifeless. This backwater which he had chosen for its quiet appearance and homely elegance was no backwater at all. Under the quiet surface, deep down, the currents moved so strongly that people were being torn away from their moorings and hurled this way and that; even Markham, whom nothing had shaken during their years of companionship, was groping like a child in the dark, and as frightened as most children. He had heard some woman crying! That was purely a question of fact. A woman must have cried for him to hear her. Of course, it was plainly Mrs. Cumming unless it was Paula whom Mr. Prentice now remembered was crying when Markham had rushed in on him the previous night. But surely he could distinguish the direction and the modulation of the cry. Or had no woman cried, and his ears had played him a trick?

Mr. Prentice acknowledged to himself that whatever the truth of Markham's confession his odd behaviour had done nothing to diminish his own anxiety; and he realized that that had been increased in proportion to the knowledge he had gained of the anxieties of his neighbours. Markham saw in the exodus of the men only the figure of his own solitude, and the face frightened him; but Mr. Prentice felt the torment of their souls beating about him and, though he had no fear of the supernatural, he found his uneasiness growing mightily so that the query which he had put to himself unthinkingly had now assumed the outline of a gigantic question mark. It had now become just as important to him as it had to any of the people who had known her intimately that he should discover where Iris was. The confusion, the distress and the anger that held the little houses and their inhabitants in bondage, all had their roots in the absence of Iris. Without her there was seemingly no rudder and the ship bucketed and whirled in a ceaseless eddy.

Mr. Prentice went up to his bedroom earlier than usual, but noted on seeing the light under his door that Markham had preceded him. Again he caught himself looking curiously around; he did not know what he expected to see and, indeed, he saw nothing that was strange, nothing that was out of place. Yet he felt he was not alone, a feeling for which he blamed Markham and, not for the first time, acknowledged the power of suggestion. He deliberately took a long time to undress and marched to and from the bathroom with slow and measured steps, confident that Markham would be listening and hoping in a vague way that his apparent calmness might engender peace about him. But when at last he got into bed and turned out the light, he didn't sleep; or thought he didn't.

Suddenly it seemed to him that he became sharply awake, and faintly in the dark he heard the sound of crying. It was not an uncontrolled, wild lamentation, but a soft, plaintive grief and Mr. Prentice found himself the more affected by it. The low sobbing tore at his heart and the misery of the voice momentarily overwhelmed him. He knew that he was overhearing no transient sorrow, but the anguish of a soul threshing weakly in the net of suffering.

After what was really only a matter of seconds, but what appeared to Mr. Prentice to be an eternity, he cautiously rose from his bed and, drawing aside as quickly as he could first the curtains and then his blind, he looked out into the courtyard. He was aware that the crying had ceased and the tranquillity of the moonlit night cradled him an instant in its primeval arms. Now for a moment in time he walked again in beauty. Slowly his eyes fell away from the ash tree and, as he leaned further out of his window, he saw standing by the marigolds, almost directly under him, the slight figure of a woman. In the silver sheen of the moon, her upturned, startled face looked pinched and white. For a moment they gazed at each other and then, without a word, she slipped away, running with grace through the gateway.

Mr. Prentice looked after her, remembering her delicate air and wondering at the litheness of her small body and the tears that had stood upon her lashes. Then he slowly first let go the blind and then the curtain, shutting out the love-liness of the night, and climbed into bed. He was anxious to turn over his curious experience in his mind, but he fell asleep at once and no dream walked.

In the morning, after having asked Markham whether he had had a good night and being assured that he had, Mr. Prentice forebore to say anything to him about his own experiences which, in the bright light of day, began to take a more indefinite outline. Not that the small, lithe figure of the woman or the quality of her features, pretty as fine porcelain, had become unsubstantial, but his own actions began to engender doubts. Had he really been awakened by her crying? Had he really left his bed to catch the elfin glance? Had he really watched the shy retreat? Or had the episode been a vivid dream? He could not be quite certain. He had thought himself awake when he had heard the crying, but he knew himself now to have been asleep and he wondered whether he had, in fact, ever become conscious; or if he had lain all the time lapped in those vivid waters which wash the shores of the mind when it is upon the threshold of returning reason.

Markham had heard nothing and Markham, whose customary gait had been so upset, should have heard because he was waiting for just such sounds and was afraid of them. Also, though so much was vivid and appeared to bear the hallmark of reality, there was much that was indistinct and the outline was growing less defined the farther the day advanced until, when he returned home in the early afternoon, all that remained clear and cogent was the face, full of sorrow, upturned above the marigolds in the cold, silver peace of the moon.

"Will you get out my blue suit?" he asked Markham the moment he had entered the house.

"Your blue suit," Markham replied. "What for?"

"I intend to pay a call," Mr. Prentice answered, "and I don't intend to pay it in the livery of a barrister or a city man or whatever a black coat and striped trousers represent."

Markham looked at him without favour.

"Mrs. Dawson's away. I told you so yesterday," he said.

"I am going to fulfil a social obligation," Mr. Prentice said. "I have been called upon and I intend to repay it."

"Mr. Fawcett's still away," Markham replied obstinately. "At any rate, I haven't seen him come back," he added.

"I hope he hasn't," Mr. Prentice said. "I intend to call on Mrs. Fawcett. I find women much better fun when their husbands aren't there."

"If you can get any fun out of Mrs. Fawcett you'll be very lucky," Markham said, but he went away to lay out Mr. Prentice's blue suit while Mr. Prentice thought what he should find to say to Mrs. Fawcett, provided she were in and didn't shut the door in his face. He knew that he had no real desire to make her acquaintance at all; it was unalloyed curiosity which was driving him on, and though he felt ashamed of his weakness he had no mind to curb it.

It was necessary for him to try and get to know Mrs. Fawcett if his knowledge of the circle of people immediately around Iris was to be complete; though he admitted to himself that no one so far had been at all helpful about the man who lived in Number 2. But he really appeared to be a young man who did keep himself to himself, and there had been no suggestion from anyone that he had taken any interest in any of them, except to complain about the noise that Paula had made lately.

Clad in his blue suit which looked surprisingly new although it was surprisingly old, Mr. Prentice fretted in his study and impatiently awaited the time to advance to such a moment when he could properly cross the courtyard and ring the bell of Number 5. Though he had never really considered Mrs. Fawcett before she suddenly became a person of no small importance, and it occurred to him that as she was apparently outside the emotional eddies and stood, so to speak, on the bank of the pool which had been so harshly whipped by the gale of circumstance she might, if she had a mind to, give him a fresh viewpoint certainly upon her husband and perhaps on everyone else. She and her husband were, after all, the oldest inhabitants.

Ten minutes before he should have gone he went and, not without a certain self-consciousness as if the eyes of everyone in the courtyard were upon him, sidled his way past his marigolds and past the wall at the end to find himself, apparently much surprised at the fact, standing outside the door of Number 5. Once there he rang the bell nervously and waited, uncomfortable and hot, not with the heat of the day but with his own embarrassment. The door opened slowly and he found himself looking down into a gentle questioning face wreathed by tidy, grey hair. There was in the narrow shoulders a suspicion of a hump and the thin body was bent a little with rheumatism.

"Mrs. Fawcett?" Mr. Prentice began, his confiding smile breaking out over his pink and genial countenance.

"Yes," she answered simply and, without fully opening the door, waited for him to continue.

"Mr. Fawcett was kind enough to call on me the other

day," he went on. "It was very nice of him as I am a new-comer to St. Anne's Court. I thought I'd repay his kindness by calling on him."

"I am afraid Mr. Fawcett is away," she said. "He had some urgent business to attend to in Cornwall."

"I am fortunate in finding you at home," Mr. Prentice replied urbanely. "To tell you the truth I am not very good at paying calls. I've never known quite what to do."

Mrs. Fawcett smiled at him, a pale and unsubstantial smile and, plainly influenced by the seeming helplessness of Mr. Prentice, held the door open a little wider so that he could come into the house if he wanted.

"If I may do the duties for my husband——" she began.

"You are certain I am not inconveniencing you?" Mr. Prentice interrupted her as he pushed his portly frame into the hall.

"Not in the least," she said. "I expect you'll know where to find our sitting-room. I believe all the houses are built on the same plan."

Mr. Prentice took the first door on his right and entered a room which was so full of furniture and knick-knacks that, for a moment, he was rather at a loss where to stand without upsetting something. Mrs. Fawcett recognized his dilemma.

"I'm afraid the room is rather full," she apologized. "One has so many treasures——"

"'Lay not up for yourselves treasures upon earth,'" Mr. Prentice interrupted her lightly; but the effect was not the one he had intended because Mrs. Fawcett immediately looked very frightened until she saw that her guest was smiling.

"I thought for a moment," she said, "that you were serious. I'm very much afraid that Mr. Fawcett would not approve of such levity. Sit over there, won't you?" she went on, indicating an armchair whose arms were covered with white linen hoods and whose back had an antimacassar stretched along its length. Wedged in this with his feet jostling a foot-stool and his arms held tightly to his sides in case he upset two show cases, one on either side, which were filled with apostle spoons, cameos, silver coins, snuff boxes and other bits and pieces of no usefulness, Mr. Prentice watched the little old woman carefully sit herself down on the chair on the opposite side of the fireplace where a large glass firescreen protected its piece of silk needlework. Mr. Prentice noted that she was wearing what was plainly the dress that he had had already described to him and that, indeed, she did look bloodless and inconsequent like a moth.

"So you have taken Number 6," she began.

"Yes, the house that used to belong to Lady Iris Todhunter," he said deliberately.

The old lady—Mr. Prentice caught himself thinking of her as such though he felt that she was not so old as she looked, peered at him out of a pair of weak and watery blue eyes.

"You were fortunate to get it," she replied. "But perhaps you knew Lady Iris."

"No, it was just chance," Mr. Prentice answered. "She seems to have been rather an extraordinary woman," he went on in a light conversational tone.

"Did my husband tell you that?" Mrs. Fawcett asked him. She gave Mr. Prentice the idea that she wouldn't have been surprised if her husband had told him so.

"Not exactly," Mr. Prentice said carefully. "But I did gather that she had made a great impression on him. And I didn't think, perhaps, that many people made that. I should have thought it was the other way round."

Mrs. Fawcett seemed to grow smaller than ever and to shrink into the lap of her armchair. She became a wisp of greyness and Mr. Prentice, noticing her hands for the first time, saw that the joints were knotted a little with arthritis and that the heavy gold band of her wedding ring would never be pulled off again.

"Yes," she whispered more to herself, it seemed to Mr. Prentice, than to answer him, "she has made a great impression on him. She's a very wonderful person, but I wish——" she stopped abruptly and looked uncertainly at Mr. Prentice as if she had been guilty of giving away some confidence to a stranger.

"You knew her yourself, of course." Mr. Prentice hastened into the silence lest the vein of conversation should peter.

E

Mrs. Fawcett sat up again and her bent frame straightened; all the aggression of which her slight body was capable was expressed by the tenseness of her form, the still, closely-knitted figure and the poor prominence of her flat chest.

"Yes, I met her," she replied.

"Perhaps you can tell me what she was like—to look at, I mean," Mr. Prentice continued in easy, light tones. "Not that I really care very much, but she keeps cropping up in conversation. I mean with the rest of our neighbours."

"I am not surprised," Mrs. Fawcett said, "though I don't know any of our neighbours very well—except by sight, of course. They don't call here, though I believe Mr. Fawcett has called on them. I expect he has frightened them," she went on. "He can be very frightening. I don't think he realizes sometimes how——" she broke off, "but he's a good man," she finished in a stronger voice, "a man of simple convictions. He doesn't understand half measures. Things are either right or wrong. It's very hard to live this life as Mr. Fawcett says it ought to be lived."

"I'm afraid I don't find myself altogether in agreement with Mr. Fawcett," Mr. Prentice replied.

"Very few people do," Mrs. Fawcett admitted. "As a matter of fact, I knew you didn't. Mr. Fawcett returned here very indignantly from his visit to you. I think he called you a hedonist. He has just lately become very intolerant." Mrs. Fawcett sighed. "He was always very strict, but something or someone——" her voice died away on the air as she rose from her chair. "I'll get you a cup of tea," she went on, "and do smoke if you want to. It upsets Mr. Fawcett, but I don't mind it. Indeed, I used to like the smell of a good cigar very much."

Mr. Prentice levered himself up from his chair with great trouble only to find that by the time he had been polite Mrs. Fawcett had left the room so, as he was on his feet, he made a careful tour of this Victorian oasis but saw nothing which was of more than passing interest except two photographs in a double silver frame on a papier-mâché table. Plainly they were likenesses of Mr. and Mrs. Fawcett when young, and he was surprised to note what a sprightly young woman Mrs.

Fawcett appeared to have been; he remarked, also, the thin-lipped, ascetic young man who had been Mr. Fawcett, and he gave a little shiver of disapproval. "Rabelais laughed in his easy chair," he muttered to himself, "and so did Zeus, but not this young man," and he felt the awakening of pity for Mrs. Fawcett. Her husband had turned the little butterfly into a moth. Perhaps she had not cared overmuch about that, but in the late afternoon of life her husband's intolerance had mounted so fast that she had discovered herself out of sympathy with him; something or someone had tipped the scale. Mr. Prentice found himself back by his armchair and gingerly resumed his seat. He had scarcely done so when Mrs. Fawcett reappeared carrying a silver tray with a silver tea service, all of which shone with careful attention, and he managed to rise again in time to place it for her on the tea table which she dragged out from under a cabinet, full to overflowing with china, and unfolded. After she had poured out the tea and handed him a cup Mr. Prentice, who was finding great difficulty in balancing the cup and eating a thin slice of bread and butter, came back to the purpose of his visit.

"You were going to tell me what Lady Iris was really like," he began.

"I don't know why you should say was," Mrs. Fawcett said. "I don't expect she has altered much in a few weeks. If it comes to that I don't suppose she'll alter much in a few years." Mr. Prentice was about to ask her why when she continued in an even, low tone of voice in which there was no trace of either enthusiasm or rancour. "Some of us—the majority of us—grow old; but there are those, both men and women, whom time misses out." She gave him a quiet little smile. "And, of course, women, if they have a mind to it, can make time do quite a lot of missing. However, I don't think Lady Iris did that—I shouldn't like you to think that."

"I think a woman is entitled to take any advantage she can," Mr. Prentice remarked, and the disturbing question of the colour of Lottie Spate's hair bobbed up and grinned at him.

"Mr. Fawcett wouldn't agree with you, I'm afraid. He thinks that all aids to beauty are so much evidence of vanity and the preacher has told us all about that," she said, but Mr. Prentice noticed that she did not say what she thought about it herself.

"When I said that time seemed to make no difference to Lady Iris, I didn't mean to imply that I had known her long," she went on, "but that she is not a young woman."

"Not a young woman!" Mr. Prentice exclaimed in surprise.

"I should put her in the middle thirties," Mrs. Fawcett said. "And now I suppose you think I am being a little unfair—a little catty," she added, using the word with faint disapproval, "but I am not; I am really full of admiration for her looks. She is a very small person——"

"Ah!" Mr. Prentice interrupted and Mrs. Fawcett looked at him, a little taken aback by the interruption, but as he seemed very interested and had plainly no immediate intention of saying anything further, she continued.

"I should say about five feet two or three and has the figure of a boy. There is something extremely"—she hesitated—"virginal about her," she went on hurriedly as if she disliked the word, "and everything about her is neat and trim, including her dark head of hair. She is like a miniature of a woman, but there is no softness upon the outside. I should not care to speak about her soul. She moves with grace, with great grace, like a boy who runs very well, if you know what I mean. But it is the timelessness of her little face coupled with the age in her violet eyes that holds the secret of her attraction." She held out her hand for his teacup. "I talk too much, I am afraid," she finished, "but it's rather a treat for me to chatter. Mr. Fawcett doesn't like women who chatter."

Mr. Prentice held out his cup, not because he wanted any more tea, but because he was too taken aback by Mrs. Fawcett's unexpected flow of words and by his own conclusions to remember to refuse.

"It does one good to talk—especially of people one likes," he said.

"I don't think I ever said that I liked her," Mrs. Fawcett replied as she poured the dregs carefully into the slop bowl and began to refill his cup. "I expect you've heard strange music at some time or another; one doesn't like it, but one listens because it does things to one's heart; and when it dies away one is thankful because the beat becomes normal again and the faintness induced by the change of beat is a thing of the past."

"But sometimes the tune remains in one's head," Mr. Prentice replied, "and one rushes about trying to catch up with it and listen to it all through again, stung to frenzy by a few ill-remembered bars."

Mrs. Fawcett handed him his cup and her pale uncertain eyes looked at him with great interest.

"Sometimes one does," she acknowledged, "and there is nothing to be done about that except to wait for the fever to starve."

Mr. Prentice considered this answer while Mrs. Fawcett sat very still, her meek hands in her lap and her head motionless. She seemed to be listening for something and Mr. Prentice wondered whether she heard a snatch from the strange music, or the tune of some well-loved hymn, or nothing at all.

"You know," she said, at length, in the gossipy voice that is peculiar to women at tea tables. "St. Anne's Court was rather a happy, sunny little corner in this vexed world. True, there was the unfortunate incident of Mrs. Dawson's baby, but that might have righted itself and, in any event, she always appeared to be a very happy creature. Mr. Fawcett couldn't understand how she could be so happy with so much sin on her conscience." She paused, but Mr. Prentice felt no inclination to put in any defence and so interrupt her train of gossip. "And that nice child of hers. One never heard it cry then, whether her mother was gadding about or at home. Then Mr. Speed—of course, he always was somewhat irregular. Mr. Fawcett says he doesn't believe he has done an honest day's work in his life; but, however that may be, he was always very jolly and he never drank to excess—at any rate so far as I know. Then Mr. and Mrs. Cumming—I think she's very pretty, don't you?" But Mrs. Fawcett didn't wait for any answer and plunged ahead again immediately in her thin, reedy voice. "They were really rather sweet with their odd little tiffs and their tremendous reconciliations. Mr. Fawcett thought poor Mrs. Cumming was rather like Jezebel, but that's only because she puts on more powder and paint than she really needs. Then Lady Iris came."

"You haven't mentioned the tenant of Number 2," Mr. Prentice felt obliged to interrupt her, but he did not say anything about her omission to mention herself and her husband.

"Oh, I don't know anything about him, do you?" Mrs. Fawcett replied. Mr. Prentice shook his head. "Mr. Fawcett has called several times on him, but he's never in and, as he does all the housework himself—at least I suppose he does, because there's no maid of any kind—Mr. Fawcett has never even seen inside the house. He appears to prefer to do his own shopping too. I saw him once with a shopping basket. A nice enough young man, but I think he's often away." She paused and looked away. "I don't think," she continued slowly, "that Lady Iris ever came into contact with him, but she did with everyone else and, immediately, there was trouble." She gave Mr. Prentice a fleeting glance from her swimming blue eyes. "A great deal of trouble one way and another," she repeated, and then her lips shut tightly.

"I understand Mr. Speed is very much attracted by her," Mr. Prentice put in diffidently, thinking there could not be much harm in saying so since Mrs. Fawcett was probably aware of it.

"Oh, you know about that, do you?" she answered; "Mr. Cumming, too, is attracted, I think." She sighed heavily.

"And——" Mr. Prentice began, but he got no further.

"Yes?" Mrs. Fawcett interrupted him, leaning forward as if she was most anxious not to miss a word; her eyes becoming strangely compelling.

"I was going to say that she seems to have upset Mrs. Dawson by being too friendly with the child," continued Mr. Prentice. Mrs. Fawcett relaxed again. "Or is it all the other way about?" Mr. Prentice asked her.

"The other way about?" Mrs. Fawcett repeated vaguely.

"I mean," he went on in quiet insistent tones, "perhaps she is sinned against and not sinning."

Mrs. Fawcett shook her head with vigour and there was no mistaking the decision of her negation.

"Mr. Fawcett had no doubt," she began, and then stopped as if she was afraid to go on; but whether she would have continued with an account of Mr. Fawcett's efforts to battle with evil or not was an alternative which was not put to the test, because both she and Mr. Prentice heard hurried foot-steps in the courtyard and instinctively they both rose to their feet at the sound of the key turning in the lock. A moment later Mr. Fawcett stood before them, his clothes hanging limply upon him and his eyes staring. Mr. Prentice was certain that there was no recognition in them and he was about to introduce himself in a conventional phrase when Mrs. Fawcett, moving forward, laid a timid hand on her husband's sleeve.

"You mustn't get overwrought like this," she said. "Give me your hat and bag and sit down. I'll make some more tea. I expect you'd be glad of it. You know Mr. Prentice, don't you? We've been having a nice cosy gossip."

"Gossip!" Mr. Fawcett exclaimed. "That's all you do, chatter. While all around you the world lies shackled in weeds." He thrust his hat and bag at her and, as she scurried out of the room, bent his tall figure towards Mr. Prentice, regarding him much as the hovering hawk regards its prey.

"Did you have a successful journey?" Mr. Prentice asked.

"No." Mr. Fawcett said.

"'What went ye out for to seek? A reed shaken by the wind?'" Mr. Prentice asked lightly.

Mr. Fawcett drew himself up to his full height and, pointing a bony and shaking finger at him, shot him a glance as fierce as any from one of the old prophets.

"Leave my house at once," he said. "You blasphemer!"

Mr. Prentice did not move at once, but when he saw Mr. Fawcett advance a step towards him he shuffled his way past the furniture and gained the hall in a quicker time than he had thought possible.

"And never come back, d'you hear?" Mr. Fawcett's voice thundered after him. "Never come back."

As Mr. Prentice closed the front door hastily behind him, he heard the uncertain steps of Mrs. Fawcett as she came from the kitchen to see what all the trouble was about, but he did not wait for explanations and, crossing the courtyard quickly, shut his own door after him with relief.

He found Markham standing in his study by the window.

"Your call doesn't seem to have been very successful," he commented gloomily. "I don't understand why you wanted to go, and in your blue suit, too."

Mr. Prentice fondled the dog for a moment as she leapt up to his knees.

"On the contrary," he replied, "it was very successful. And if Mr. Fawcett hadn't blown in on the breath of Jehovah it would have been still more so."

"He's not sane," Markham said. "At any rate, he didn't look it when he came past the window."

"Would you be sane if you'd lost what you valued most in life and didn't know where to find it?" he asked gently.

"I've nothing so valuable that I couldn't afford to lose it," Markham replied. "Anyway what has he lost that he's in such a state about it?"

"A woman has run away with his soul," he answered.

Markham stared at him and an uneasy look replaced his usual sad and dejected expression; he shivered slightly and moved away from the window.

"You shouldn't say things like that," he said, and went from the room casting a curious glance over his shoulder at Mr. Prentice who, absent-mindedly still fondling the dog, was looking at the picture of Lottie Spate on the mantelpiece.

"So it was Iris I dreamt I saw in the moonlight by the marigolds," he said to the dog as he moved towards his chair. "I knew it was really, all the time; but what was she crying for? Not crying, that's too small a word. She managed to carry an ocean of tears in the pools of her eyes."

Lottie Spate curled herself at her master's feet and returned no answer, not even a wag of the tail; but her calm and complacent attitude was far from being shared by her master whose mind was gradually being whipped until it twisted and turned to avoid the recurring blows. But twist and turn as he might, Mr. Prentice was unable to put Iris out of his thoughts and, now that he knew what she looked like, her face pressed close to his and her cry rang in his heart as lonely as the sound of a lute on a hill in Thessaly. With all the urgency that beat about him a sense of hopeless frustration went hand in hand. From those same causes he traced the incipient madness of Mr. Fawcett, the potations of Mr. Speed and the ineffective cavorting of Mr. Cumming. Was he in the grip of a crowd hysteria? Was that all there was to it? Or was he caught up in some much more esoteric and stealthy pattern? He only knew that peace of mind had fled before him down the tortuous ways of the hours, and that unless somewhere and at some time Iris reappeared or one of them found her, he was, no more than they, to rest.

He had little opportunity to put his thoughts away from him, because he had not been trying with the aid of a good book for very long when he heard an insistent ring on the front door bell. He thought wryly to himself that the very fact of his having heard it showed how little he had succeeded in concentrating upon what he was reading, and how sharpened his senses had become to extraneous matters. In the ordinary way he was sure he would never have noticed the sound, but now not only had he heard it, but his whole attention was focused on the trivial incident. He had not long to wait to find out who his visitor was for Markham showed Norman Cumming in with every appearance of distaste.

"I told Mr. Cumming you were out," Markham said, "but he said he knew better."

"As he apparently does," Mr. Prentice replied, rising to greet him.

"I'm sorry, I had to see you," Norman Cumming muttered awkwardly, his eyes on Markham as he waited for his departure.

When Markham had gone he looked at Mr. Prentice who noticed at once that the drawn expression, which he had remarked before, had increased so that now two lines ran from his cheek bones to his chin, marking clearly where the flesh had fallen away.

"You don't look very well," Mr. Prentice said with concern.

Norman Cumming pulled out his cigarette case, put a cigarette in his mouth and, nervously flicking his lighter several times, eventually lit the cigarette.

"Oh, I'm all right," he replied.

Mr. Prentice waved him towards a chair and sat down himself.

"Is there anything I can do?" he asked.

Norman Cumming sat down and flicked the, as yet non-existent, ash towards the carpet.

"I thought perhaps," he began. "I'm probably wrong," he went on, "but Joyce appeared to take a liking to you."

"I hope so," Mr. Prentice replied simply. "I like her."

"When did you see her last?"

"See her last?" Mr. Prentice repeated a little blankly. "Let me see now. Oh yes, yesterday evening. She came and had a glass of sherry with me."

"Would you mind telling me what she came to see you about, or did you ask her in yourself?"

Mr. Prentice gave the young man a shrewd look and began to think out his reply a little carefully.

"Or perhaps you'd rather not," Norman Cumming went on. "If you'd rather not it doesn't matter."

"What is it, exactly, you want to know?" Mr. Prentice asked.

Norman Cumming raised his eyes to him doggedly.

"I want to know whether she said anything about going away, and if so whether she said where she was going," he answered.

"You mean that she isn't at home?" Mr. Prentice jerked out in involuntary surprise.

Norman Cumming rose to his feet.

"No, she isn't," he snapped back. "But you obviously know nothing about it. It was just a chance. I'm sorry to have worried you." He took a few quick nervous strides towards the door.

"You haven't worried me," Mr. Prentice said gently. "Why not sit down? I may be able to help a little."

Norman Cumming swung round again.

"I don't see how," he replied.

"I gather she has gone away and left no address," Mr. Prentice said.

Norman Cumming hesitated a moment.

"Yes," he answered.

"I thought she might, but I hoped I had persuaded her to stay where she was a little longer," Mr. Prentice replied.

"She did tell you she would?"

Mr. Prentice nodded.

"With anyone else?" Norman Cumming muttered.

"No one else was mentioned," Mr. Prentice said. "I don't think so. In fact, I think she's very fond of you. Only she's very young." As he said that Mr. Prentice had no image of Joyce Cumming in his mind, but he saw instead the bent and thin figure of Mrs. Fawcett. "If she had been older she would have waited longer— perhaps for ever. Women have waited, you know," he added.

Norman Cumming flung himself down in his chair again.

"Oh, I don't blame her," he burst out.

Mr. Prentice got up and put his hand towards the bell.

"You'll stay to dinner?" he said. "I don't expect there's anything prepared for you in your place."

"It's very kind of you," Norman Cumming replied, jumping to his feet once more. "But thank you, no. I must be getting along."

Mr. Prentice let his hand fall without ringing the bell.

"I don't think you'll find her," he said very deliberately.

"I am not going to look," Norman Cumming replied. "Joyce is quite within her rights. It's only I'd like to have had a word with her before she went, that's all."

"I wasn't referring to your wife," Mr. Prentice said. "I think she'll come back when she finds you are home for good."

Norman Cumming looked uncomfortable.

"I don't know what you mean," he muttered.

"I don't think you'll find Lady Iris," Mr. Prentice said.

"Why the devil not?" Norman Cumming flashed back, in his surprise not troubling to beat about the bush any longer.

"Because I don't think she wants to be found by you," Mr. Prentice replied. "Or perhaps she is just afraid," he went on.

"Afraid of what?"

But Mr. Prentice did not answer the question; he regarded Joyce Cumming's admission to him in the light of a confidence.

"You've been looking for her all the time, haven't you?" he asked him instead. "So, I suspect, has Mr. Fawcett."

"Fawcett!" Norman Cumming exclaimed in contempt. "I shouldn't be surprised if he's at the bottom of the whole of this business. I——" he broke off abruptly. "How the devil do you know about Fawcett?" he asked.

"Mr. Speed sent him to St. Ives to find her," Mr. Prentice explained. "I think he hoped with both of you away she might be tempted back and he would be here to receive her. Only it hasn't worked out quite like that. And now Mr. Fawcett is back, and Mr. Speed is away."

Norman Cumming looked at Mr. Prentice with a new interest and a puzzled frown creased his forehead.

"You seem to have made yourself very well informed," he said. "What's the idea?"

"You've all made me curious," Mr. Prentice replied carefully. "Only I don't quite understand why you should think Mr. Fawcett should be at the bottom of the whole business, as you put it."

Norman Cumming gave him another sharp glance, stubbed his cigarette out, put his hands in his pockets and then shrugged his shoulders.

"Oh well," he replied, "I don't suppose it matters now. Nothing matters much any more unless——" He looked at Mr. Prentice defiantly. "No sooner had I fallen in love with Iris," he said, "than that long streak of righteousness went to her and threatened her with the wages of sin. He went in and out of her house like an avenging angel. At least, he did at first; afterwards it seemed to me that the—in fact, I was sure that he was going there for quite another reason." He laughed again contemptuously.

"But why should he wish to save her soul? What had she done wrong?" Mr. Prentice asked.

"Done wrong?" Norman Cumming repeated bitterly. "She's never done anything wrong, so far as I know anyway. But he couldn't make any impression on me. When a woman gets into one's blood there's no such thing as right or wrong. There is nothing and no one except her. Don't I know it!"

"And what did Lady Iris say or do?" Mr. Prentice asked him as the echo of Speed's words reverberated in his ears.

"She told him to mind his own business; but Fawcett isn't a man to take no for an answer, I'll say that for him," Norman Cumming replied. "The more she laughed at him the keener he became; until it seemed to me that her soul was the only soul in the whole wide world that he wanted to save."

"But as she hadn't done anything wrong——" Mr. Prentice began.

"Maybe; but I was not exactly idle, you know," Norman Cumming interrupted him and gave a forced laugh. "I'm not idle now from choice, if it comes to that. I've searched all those places that she has spoken of to me—wild places and lonely places that she was fond of, and searched in vain. Joyce threw her up at me and, after threatening to leave me, has left me. It's my fault; it's got nothing to do with Iris." He paused and then went on, more to himself than to his host. "There was always something that escaped me: perhaps if I could have found, or could find, all that lay behind——" He broke off abruptly and turned away towards the door. "You wouldn't understand," he said. "It's no use trying to explain things to anyone when one can't explain them to oneself. She wasn't good; but she wasn't bad."

"Perhaps she's just pagan," Mr. Prentice suggested quietly.

Norman Cumming shook his head hopelessly.

"I don't know," he said. "As a matter of fact, I don't quite know what you mean, but there things are. I've looked everywhere, I've written and I can't think what more I can do. But until I am certain inside me, one way or the other, that the end has really been reached, I shall go on looking."

"And when you find that the end has been reached?" Mr. Prentice asked.

"I can reach it as well as the next person," Norman Cumming answered and rushed from the room and out of the house into the golden sunset. Mr. Prentice looked after him and thought of his wife and the revolver; but as the end was plainly not yet and Joyce had told him that she had hidden the revolver with some care, he did not find himself unduly anxious.

Dimly now he began to see, or thought he could discern, the faint outline of a pattern, but the centre was indistinct and blurred and he hoped for his own sake, and still more for the sake of the people more closely tied to the fleet feet of Iris, that the end would not be overlong delayed. As the scant details passed in vague review before him and he began to set his disordered thoughts in order and to rally his mind, he found his previous agitation leaving him to be replaced by something akin to tranquillity. He started to experience a lofty detachment and, while still disturbed by the troubles of his neighbours, their agitation no longer influenced him so that he, in turn, lost his self-control. Now he waited calmly, realizing that there was nothing he could do but wait.

Whether it was because of this new mental approach to the enigma of the disappearance of Iris, or whether it was because neither Mr. Fawcett nor Norman Cumming nor any other person came to see him on the Sunday, or whether it was that Markham appeared, at any rate momentarily, to have recovered his former poise, he found Sunday a day much as other Sundays had been in his life, and no side wind harried the towers of his mind. He did not see Mr. Fawcett's angular figure, his head thrust forward and his eyes burning with the fever of hidden fires, stride down the court to church. He did not see the timid glance which Mrs. Fawcett, following in her husband's wake, threw at his marigolds. He did not see because he did not look. Nor did he dig up some excuse to rap on the house next door to find out whether Norman Cumming had searched for the revolver—and searched in vain; nor did he hear him slam the front door in impatient rage. He didn't hear him because he wasn't listening. All those events belonged to the pattern, but they were part of the bold border and that was nearly completed; it was the centre which held his attention and upon which he gazed, trying to make out the details and determined to keep his eyes from blinking so that his sight should be unimpaired. So far as he could be sure about anything, however, he thought it certain that there was no chance that he would himself become a part of the border, the outline of which he had so curiously nearly completed. There must be some relationship between the border and the centre.

It is sometimes not easy to find the key or formulate the exact reason why a design, viewed as a whole, is satisfactory, or to recognize precisely the fashion in which the parts are correlated to the whole. The clue may lie in the colours and their use, or in the drawing or in the combination of the two, whereby the subject is presented with a fullness that is satisfying as it is complete. Mr. Prentice, although he had sketched out the border with some boldness in his mind and had an indistinct impression of the centre of the mould, had not so far succeeded in finding any link between the two. That there must be such a link he was quite certain and it was with a flush, first of pleasure and then of astonishment, that he listened to the welcome of his clerk when he arrived at his chambers on the Monday morning.

"I've got good news for you, sir," the clerk said as he came into Mr. Prentice's room after they had exchanged the customary good morning in the outer office. "Mr. Staines of Lawford, Foy and Cross telephoned me first thing this morning. They want to come and see you to-morrow afternoon at 4.30."

"What's it all about?" Mr. Prentice asked.

"I gather it's about a right of way," his clerk replied. "As far as I can gather the Council is going for the Earl of Rawton for a declaration that there is a right of way over his lordship's property." The clerk smiled. "You wanted a big case; here it is, I think. Unless there's a settlement," he added gloomily.

But Mr. Prentice, whose attention had been caught and held a moment by the name of the firm of solicitors for whom, so far as he knew, he had never acted before and whose business was very considerable, ceased to think about the implications of the action as outlined by his clerk, the moment he had heard the name of Lord Rawton. This was, he felt, no fantastic coincidence; and he waited for his clerk to leave him so that he could puzzle out the implications, but his clerk didn't go and he became aware that he was saying something further which was very much to the point.

"The only thing is that Lord Rawton is very anxious for you to go up to Rawton Hall," he went on. "I gather he wants you to see the disputed right of way. I gather, also, that it isn't convenient for his lordship to come to town at the moment. Of course, as Mr. Staines said, Mr. Lawford thinks it all rather unnecessary, but also thinks, unless you really can't spare the time, it would be wiser to fall in with his lordship's wishes, especially as he particularly asked for you to be briefed in the matter."

"Ah!" Mr. Prentice exclaimed. "I shall certainly go, of course," he added.

The clerk was a little taken aback by his forthright acceptance of the situation.

"The sooner the better, too," Mr. Prentice continued. "What have I got on to-day?"

"Nothing very much," the clerk answered. "I mean, I could put off the two conferences this afternoon: but hadn't you better wait, sir, until you've seen Mr. Lawford?"

Mr. Prentice shook his head vigorously.

"I think that's quite unnecessary," he replied. "You ring them up and say I am quite prepared to go to-day for the night, if it suits his lordship, and they can make the necessary arrangements for me."

The clerk hesitated a moment.

"As you like, sir," he replied at length.

At four-fifteen that afternoon Mr. Prentice found the lodge gates of Rawton Hall opening for him on their creaking rusty hinges and, as he drove up in a hired car over the potholed surface of the drive, a feeling of excitement welled up inside him which had nothing to do with the issues involved in the case or the unexpected windfall that had come his way.

All this had not been accomplished without trouble. The solicitors had disliked being bustled and it was through some consistent lying by his clerk, instigated and insisted upon by

Mr. Prentice, that Mr. Lawford had been prevailed upon to telephone his lordship to tell him that Monday and Tuesday were the only days that Mr. Prentice could spare for a very long time. Lord Rawton, however, far from being upset at the short notice had welcomed the suggestion. He had expressed down the telephone his poor opinion of the Council, his desire to get on with the whole unsavoury business as soon as possible and his thanks to Mr. Prentice for the promptness of his conduct; but Markham had been quite another matter. He had packed up a bag for his master, had brought it along to his chambers and, once there, had insisted on seeing him.

"How long are you away for?" he had asked.

"Until to-morrow," Mr. Prentice had replied.

"I am not staying in the house alone at night, nor's the dog," Markham had said.

It had been on the tip of Mr. Prentice's tongue to press for a reason and to insist on his staying, but after a moment's thought, much to Markham's surprise, he had given way.

"Very well," he had said. "But where will you go?"

"My sister's."

Mr. Prentice had looked at him a little astonished.

"I didn't know you had a sister," he had said.

"Well, I have." And on that very positive affirmative the short interview had closed.

Markham's behaviour and that of Lord Rawton had fully occupied the mind of Mr. Prentice on his way down. What had moved his lordship to ask his solicitors particularly to brief him and thus allow him not only to view the immediate future with more confidence, but what for some reason he regarded as much more important, to enter the house of Lady Iris? Here was the link which he had never thought would be forged and he saw now that it was he himself who was the key to the pattern—the bridge between the border and the centre upon which the structure stood and without which there was no unity. But he had only abstract ideas of exactly how he was going to be used.

As the car wobbled along the weedy drive, Mr. Prentice looked about him with curiosity and saw ahead of him another pair of wrought iron gates that guarded the entrance to the

Hall and its immediate environs. He saw the rose-red bricks which softened the lines of the centre and the two wings of the house; he saw the outline of a large lily pond, built into the courtyard itself and the idle fountain that reared its graceful head in the centre; he saw the topiary work that in ordered array graced the flagged surface and, when he drove up to the front door whose marvellous stone façade was crumbling with neglect, he felt more insignificant than he, who was never egotistical, had ever felt before.

Carrying his small, old and battered bag he stood underneath the friendly, but immense doorway and waited for someone to answer the wrought iron bell handle which he had pulled, at first with a certain timidity and the second time with more courage.

As his car was jolted away a sense of fright hemmed him in and, with a sudden wish to leave in it, he turned abruptly away from the tall portal to watch it wistfully as it swayed away into the park. "All this is too much for me," he muttered, as he stood awkwardly first on one foot and then on the other, but he did not define for himself whether by "all this" he meant the lawsuit, possibly so remunerative in comparison with his small, infrequent, briefs, or the riddle of Lady Iris.

In the stillness he heard unhurried footsteps on the marble floor inside the house and, when the door opened, saw an old man standing before him. He had a bald, high forehead, carried his spare frame with a quiet, unassuming dignity, and his eyes were grave. After one brief look at Mr. Prentice he held out a firm, long hand.

"Mr. Prentice?" he said. "I'm Lord Rawton. Come in."

Mr. Prentice, who felt his own hand to be stickier and his own figure to be more rotund and flabby than they really were, went inside, his black coat hanging awkwardly and his trousers baggy at the knees, and stood in what he saw to be a colonnade, rather than a hall, between the columns of which stood marble statues of Greece and Italy, each on its pedestal.

Mr. Prentice knew little or nothing about statuary, but he recognized some of the subjects without much difficulty and, while his host closed the door, gave them a cursory glance to find his attention at once wholly devoted to a Venus. For some reason or other he immediately began to think of Miss Lottie Spate and hastily transferred his eyes to a helmeted and fully clothed Minerva.

"My great-grandfather brought some of the collection back and acquired others here," Lord Rawton explained as he joined him. "I find the effect somewhat depressing myself. Toddy used to be rather frightened, I remember; but my daughter giggled, in fact still does, especially at that copy of the Barberini Hera." He turned and, opening a door at the end of the marble passage, waited for Mr. Prentice to follow him. "Toddy," he went on, "sent me a very enthusiastic letter about you."

Mr. Prentice stood still in astonishment but Lord Rawton, following his gaze which, in fact, was as blank as that of the Hera whom they had just left and thinking that he was lost in admiration of the grand staircase, gave him time to recover from his amazement.

"That was very nice of your son," he stammered out at length.

"He recommended you to me most warmly," Lord Rawton went on as he led the way up the staircase. "Though what Toddy was doing in the Athenæum I can't imagine. I thought he was more impressed with garters than gaiters."

"Athenæum!" echoed Mr. Prentice, to whom the conversation appeared to be more astounding than the grand sweep of the staircase.

"I gathered he had run into you by chance—a fortunate chance for me as well, I am certain," Lord Rawton continued, taking the left hand passage on the top landing where the staircase forked. "As there are virtually no servants," he went on, "there is virtually no house. I only keep four bedrooms open and, as my three children never seem to arrive together, I find that adequate. It's somewhat like living in an empty town and rather disconcerting until you're used to it."

"It's a great pity——" Mr. Prentice began.

"Oh, I'm not sorry for myself," Lord Rawton interrupted

him. "I daresay my elder boy will sell the place or hand it over for death duties, and the great British public will scatter the grounds with bottles on Bank Holidays and leave it alone every other day of the year. What I am sorry about is that all the girls and young men in the village apparently prefer to lead a stupid life in a factory to a peaceful life here. A place like this, however much trouble it may be, gives people a background; that is what people lack to-day, or so it seems to me. If one comes here one can't fail to be impregnated in some fashion with its beauty." He threw open a door. "I hope you'll be comfortable," he continued. "It's really Iris's room, but as she's so seldom here I give it to my guests now."

Mr. Prentice entered the room with a lively feeling of curiosity. He saw a low couch—at least, the piece of furniture looked more like a couch than a bed to him—whose head was raised upon two scrolls and whose legs were so short that the mattress nearly touched the floor. It was covered with a golden bedspread; and on each side of it stood two wooden chairs with golden cushions on them and high backs. In front of each chair was a golden footstool. The curtains to the long windows were also golden, and the carpet was coloured a midnight blue. Across the angle of the wall on the right of the window there was a marble table, in the centre of which was set a looking-glass supported by the figure of Hercules. Before it stood a low chair whose legs looked like an inverted pair of pincers, with leather thongs or straps for a seat. Mr. Prentice looked upward and saw that the vaulted ceiling had been painted and that upon a blue background were outlined in silver the moon and the stars.

Lord Rawton watched him as he stood in the doorway looking about him with unabashed interest.

"A few of my guests find it great fun," he observed at length.

"Fun!" Mr. Prentice exclaimed. "It's very severe— beautiful, I think."

"Well, it's different," Lord Rawton admitted, "and wrangles with the rest of the house except, perhaps, the colonnade of numbing nudes."

Mr. Prentice stepped into the room.

"What is the picture?" he asked. "The light falls on the glass from here."

Lord Rawton moved aside as Mr. Prentice made his way eagerly over the rich blue pile of the carpet so that he could see what was set in place above the marble mantelpiece. Once he had found a position to see it that satisfied him, he remained looking at it in silence for what seemed to be to his host an unconscionable time.

"You like it?" Lord Rawton ventured at last.

But Mr. Prentice did not reply, for he had found himself gazing at the face that he had seen upturned by the marigolds: a piquant, small, elfin face whose young violet eyes smiled derisively into his and from whose provoking smile there seemed to be no escape. The small mouth was alive, too, with the shadow of that same smile. But though the smile and the likeness to the sad face which he had glimpsed for a moment in the moonlight held him tongue-tied, there was one further detail in the picture which startled him more than anything else. The girl was dressed in white samite with tiny golden threads tumbling through the material; in her hand she held a staff and two golden wings sprouted from her shoulders.

Mr. Prentice thought the picture to be only about two feet six by two feet; but even so he knew it dominated the whole room and he knew, also, that the woman he had pursued in his dreams had turned to face him.

"You don't by any chance know my daughter, do you?" Lord Rawton tried again.

"So that is Lady Iris," Mr. Prentice said in a surprised tone, though he had known it all along. He withdrew his eyes with difficulty. "No, I don't," he went on, "although I have her house, you know." He smiled. "Or rather one of yours."

"Her house?" Lord Rawton echoed, a little puzzled.

"In St. Anne's Court," Mr. Prentice explained.

"Have you!" Lord Rawton said. "Toddy said nothing about that. Iris wrote to me a little time ago saying that she was giving up the lease. That's very interesting." But he didn't sound very interested. "You'll find the cupboard here empty for your things and there's a bathroom next door.

When you're ready come and join me in the library; it's the first door on the right at the bottom of the stairs." Lord Rawton gave Mr. Prentice a friendly nod and, shutting the door, left him standing between the foot of the bed and the picture in his black coat and striped trousers, holding his battered suitcase and conscious only of the clear, virginal eyes with the derisive smile.

Mr. Prentice took out of his bag the few things that he had brought with him, laid his toilet articles on the marble table in front of the mirror, threw his striped pyjamas and dressing-gown on to the gold coverlet and with one backward glance at the portrait, the eyes of which seemed to follow his every movement with an amused interest, went to join his host.

He found him in a long room, the walls of which were shelved with books from floor to ceiling; even the door by which he entered swung on a great hinge that supported an entire bookcase so that when he had shut it after him there appeared to be an unbroken line of volumes. Lord Rawton was seated at a walnut desk and before him was spread a map.

"Ah, there you are," he said. "You'll find a cup of tea over by the fireplace. Help yourself."

Mr. Prentice thanked him and moved over to the table.

"I'm sorry to have dragged you down here," Lord Rawton went on, "but I think it's better for you to know the lie of the land rather than to rely on Mr. Lawford and a map." He paused. "Briefly," he went on, "the situation is as follows. My family has for some time permitted various people from the village, whom we have known well, to make a short cut across the park so saving them a good half mile walk to get to the high road on the other side: and I daresay a number of other people have used it without permission, but they behaved themselves. When the war broke out, however, a couple of factories were built near here with the result that a great many unauthorized persons made use of it." He shrugged his shoulders. "Well, there was a war on and it did save them a good deal of time, so I did nothing about it, but their manners were not of the best and in any case there is now no war on. I, therefore, decided to close the path to everyone for the time being, but the Council have thought fit to claim that this path is a right of way."

Mr. Prentice, who had poured out his tea and was munching a piece of bread and butter, did his utmost to pay every attention to the remarks of his host, but he did not find it very easy. In fact, after a little while, although he nodded his head sagely, studied the map of the estate at his lordship's request, made the appropriate noises at what he hoped were the appropriate places, his attention wandered in the most reprehensible manner.

"Well, there it all is," Lord Rawton finished at length. "I daresay Lawford will instruct you with more precision, but I thought it better for you to have the outline of the story from me personally, and to have a look at the lie of the land for yourself."

"I'm very much obliged to you," Mr. Prentice said. "I'll talk a walk over the path myself, if I may."

"I was about to suggest it," Lord Rawton replied and, leading the way from the library, went before him into the colonnade of statues. Here, at the feet of Artemis, Mr. Prentice found his homburg hat, but he also found something else which he had overlooked in the flurry of his arrival. Near it on the same table was a pile of letters. As he picked up his hat he couldn't help seeing that they were addressed to Lady Iris. Standing timidly near the table and twiddling his hat in his fingers, he cleared his throat nervously.

"Lady Iris is away?" he asked diffidently.

Lord Rawton's somewhat aloof, though friendly, expression, became more aloof and a little less companionable. He merely nodded and led the way out of the house.

"I only asked because I wondered whether you knew her address," Mr. Prentice continued, as he pattered after his lordship whose long strides made it impossible for him to keep in step. "I—er—have a letter to forward and I wondered where to send it."

"You'd better send it here," Lord Rawton said.

"Is she away for long?" Mr. Prentice asked.

"I haven't the least idea," Lord Rawton replied. "Iris is a law to herself. For that matter so are most children to-day so far as I can make out from the gossip of my tenants. All the same," he went on with a touch of anger, "I wish she wouldn't disappear without leaving any address. It only means that I have to answer the telephone to every Tom, Dick and Harry who wants to get hold of her."

Mr. Prentice thought about Mr. Fawcett, Mr. Speed and Mr. Cumming, but he did not mention their names.

"She likes to go away by herself?" he put in conversationally.

"Iris has always been a little out of the ordinary," Lord Rawton said without enthusiasm. "That room of hers is hardly usual," he went on as if to defend his point of view against any argument.

"Who painted her picture?" Mr. Prentice asked.

"She painted it herself, of course," Lord Rawton answered in surprised tones; then noting Mr. Prentice's look of astonishment went on. "Oh, I forgot you didn't know her. Not that she paints anything now, so far as I know. Yes, she painted that when she was sixteen, and the ceiling as well."

"When she was sixteen!" Mr. Prentice exclaimed.

"But though she gave herself wings, she was far from being an angel," Lord Rawton went on a little grimly.

"You've no idea when she's coming back, I suppose?" Mr. Prentice asked in a somewhat bolder voice.

"None whatever." Lord Rawton's denial was flat and made in a tone wholly without interest. "Now, here is the path," he went on with a great deal more animation, and they stood upon it while he explained exactly where it came and whither it was going. "I've got to go and see one of my tenants," he went on. "I don't suppose you'll want to do that——" he paused.

"I'll take a walk down the path, if I may," Mr. Prentice put in, "and have a look at the village."

"That's a very good idea," Lord Rawton agreed heartily, and Mr. Prentice had no difficulty in realizing that he would be glad to be rid of him. "When you get to the end of the path you'll find it barricaded up, but go along the hedge to your right and you'll find a hole. I use that way myself now. We dine about half-past seven."

Mr. Prentice, who hadn't brought a dinner jacket and wondered whether he ought to have done so, went off a little gloomily; but such trivialities did not bother him for long; nor did the purpose of his visit, though he did note that the path was well worn from long usage. Finding the hole in the hedge, he scrambled through and emerged in the village street. Facing him he saw the Rawton Arms and, with a brief glance up and down the winding road, walked across it and entered the saloon bar. The place was as clean as a newly-minted penny and behind the bar sat an old woman with kind, clear eyes who looked more likely to give a customer a pint of milk than any alcoholic drink. She eyed Mr. Prentice with bright curiosity and asked him what he wanted. When later she heard that he was staying at the Hall her interest became still more marked.

"And how is his lordship?" she asked. "Worried, I expect."

"Worried?" Mr. Prentice echoed.

"This case and everything," she explained. "He's always been very good to the village. People only have to ask him, you know. He'd give them anything, but he won't have things taken. The war brought a lot of strangers here." She sighed and lapsed into silence as she contemplated the change.

"You know the Hall well, I expect?" Mr. Prentice said.

The old woman smiled.

"I should," she answered. "I was nurse there before I married Mr. Huggins, after Master Edward went to school."

"I met him in London," Mr. Prentice answered quickly as he studied the old lady with greater care.

"Did you now?" she answered. "He's a nice young man, but he doesn't come in here very often now. Times have changed. I sometimes wonder whether anyone knows exactly where they're going. Mr. Huggins was only saying yesterday everyone seems to have more money to spend, but they don't get a quarter the value for it. It doesn't make any sense, he says."

Mr. Prentice agreed that it didn't and, only with difficulty, prevented himself from going into a long dissertation on the cost of living, the value of the shilling and other kindred matters.

"Is Lady Iris at the Hall?" the old lady asked; but her voice had lost its frankness. It was as if she didn't want to put the question and yet had been impelled to do so in spite of herself.

"No," Mr. Prentice replied. "She's gone away somewhere, I believe," he added vaguely. "As a matter of fact, I've got her room."

The old lady looked at him sharply and as quickly dropped her eyes again.

"It's a very odd room, don't you think?" Mr. Prentice said after a short silence.

"Lady Iris is rather an odd person," she replied. "But I shouldn't say that," she went on almost at once. "Besides it's not really her fault, poor little lamb."

"Not her fault?" Mr. Prentice repeated encouragingly as he pushed his empty glass forward for the old lady to refill it; but she didn't answer him as she took it from him and refilled it with sherry from a bottle on the shelf.

"In what way is Lady Iris odd?" he tried again, after he had watched her for a moment or two gazing into space and apparently unaware of his presence. She appeared startled at his interruption and glanced round the deserted bar as if to make sure they were alone.

"You mustn't get me gossiping," she answered.

"She must have been a very pretty child," he prodded her memory relentlessly.

"She was; oh, she was," the old lady said enthusiastically, "but"—she paused a moment—"her mother died in giving birth to her. Lord Rawton's been married twice."

"And the second Lady Rawton?"

"Master Edward's mother? She ran away. He divorced her for desertion." The old lady's lips set in a thin line; it was plain to Mr. Prentice that she did not approve.

"I didn't know," he said. "She ran away!" he went on in a surprised voice. "I shouldn't have thought that his lordship was——"

"He's had a very sad life," she interrupted him. She sighed

and taking up a duster began to wipe the counter as if it was dirty. "I expect the Hall will go when Master Henry succeeds and then we'll have trippers and noises, if this lawsuit doesn't bring them here earlier. Lady Iris won't like it. She never liked company much, even as a child."

"You were her nurse as well as Master Edward's?" Mr. Prentice asked, trying to put no emphasis into his question, but he was aware of his own excitement as he awaited her reply.

The old lady nodded.

"Yes, and a nice troublesome child she was," she answered. "Always making mischief; but she was very clever. She drew beautifully and played, too; but such odd things. His lordship couldn't make head or tail of her, but then he didn't try very hard." Her lips came together again and marked by their uncompromising line her disapproval.

"Didn't he like her, then?"

The old lady shook her head.

"It seems a little unreasonable of him," Mr. Prentice went on gently.

"It appeared so to me," the old lady answered candidly. "But then——" she shrugged her shoulders.

"But he must have had a reason," Mr. Prentice persisted. "I shouldn't like you to think that Lord Rawton was unkind for no reason at all. In any case it was only at the beginning," the old lady said hastily. "He's always been very good to Mr. Huggins and me. I never believed what he did, you see."

Mr. Prentice looked puzzled and waited with what patience he could command while he watched the wavering expression in her face, and sensed that she was having a battle with her conscience whether she should say anything further, or remain silent. Judging that he was more likely to hear something more if he kept his own tongue quiet, he said nothing.

"Well, it's an old story now," the old lady began at length, "and I don't suppose it really matters much. Anyway I never believed it," she went on with a touch of defiance. "Only his lordship was away abroad for some time and, when he came back and found that her ladyship was"—she hesitated—"with child, he didn't believe it was his, and though he didn't turn her out they didn't speak, and then when Lady Iris was born she died; and I don't think his lordship ever forgave himself. And, at first, he disliked the poor lamb. Afterwards he tried to make it up to her, but he's never really understood her, and she's always away."

Mr. Prentice took a little time to digest all this, and the old woman, who had rattled over the cobbles of the story as if glad to part with it as quickly as she could, relapsed into silence upon a sigh like a spent wind in the poplars.

"But he married again?" he said at length.

"Oh yes," the old woman replied rather indifferently, "he married again; but she couldn't get on with Lady Iris either, and in any case I don't think his lordship——" she broke off again, but Mr. Prentice had no trouble in completing the unfinished sentence for himself.

"How old is Lady Iris?" he asked.

"She was born in 1914," she said without hesitation. "I shall never forget it. In the morning, it was about ten o'clock. There was a terrible thunderstorm, I remember, and then the sun came out and Lady Iris was crying in my arms and her ladyship was dead. They went for his lordship, but he was too late." She paused. "When Lady Iris painted her room, just before Master Edward went to school, she put in one extra bright star on the ceiling. You'll see it, no doubt," she went on. " 'That,' she told me, 'is my mother'."

Mr. Prentice remembered the star, but his stream of information was quickly dammed by the arrival of a party of motorists to whom the old lady took their drinks and an obvious dislike. It was plain to Mr. Prentice that tales from the Hall were "not for the likes of them," and that he had heard all that he was going to hear that evening; so he finished his sherry, paid for it and, bidding her good-night, crawled with some discomfort once more through the hole in the hedge with the uncomfortable feeling that his acrobatics were being watched by half the village.

But once in the park, his face turned towards the house which stood in a hollow, and so guarded by trees that he could only see the tops of the roofs.

"From time immemorial" was a phrase which Mr. Prentice had associated with the reign of Richard the First for so long a period that he had been in danger of forgetting that the arbitrary limitation was merely a legal maxim. Now he was struck by the girth of the oaks and the immutability which their presence conveyed.

Below him, to his right, stretched a large, reedy mere and, as he left the footpath to stand upon its edge, he felt himself overlooked by the infinite and the chilling sleeve of eternity brushed against his face. He thought himself to be alone with the beginning, so still was everything, and a panic fanned by the Great God with the goat's feet blew about his heart. For an instant, he stood with frightened eyes looking over the still rushes in the grey evening, then he hurried away up the hill, leaving the fearful riddle behind him and not daring to look back in case he should glimpse the mystery to die in terror; while all around him the oaks, the giant outposts of time, stood motionless.

He came, at length, to the Hall and was surprised to find that his heart was beating fast as if he had run a long way, and his hands were damp with sweat and his throat dry as if he had been out in the heat of a summer day. Without looking at the statuary, he hastily put his hat on the table and, wheeling abruptly at the foot of the grand staircase turned the handle of the library door and, entering, felt that he had reached sanctuary. A lone figure, lounging in an armchair, surveyed him languidly.

"Hullo, I heard you were down already," Toddy said. Mr. Prentice recovered his balance with a jerk and hoped that nothing of what he was really feeling showed on his face.

"Where's father, do you know?" Toddy went on, and his further question gave Mr. Prentice time to complete his descent to the world of the moment.

"He went to have a word with one of his tenants," he said. "I must say I am very indebted to you."

"Indebted to me? What for?"

"Recommending me to your father," Mr. Prentice answered. "It was a very kind thought on your part."

Mr. Prentice looked so genuinely pleased and affected that Toddy became a little embarrassed.

"Not at all, not at all," he replied. "As a matter of fact, I hadn't much to do with it really. It was Violette. She appears to think you're about the only decent person she has met and she's very touched by your interest in her late mother." He paused. "To tell you the truth, I didn't think the old man would take any notice—I expect it was the mention of the Athenæum that did it," he chuckled.

"It seemed to me rather an odd place for me to meet you," Mr. Prentice agreed. "I think your father thought so too."

"Well, I'm glad it came off," Toddy said, "though I hardly expected to find you up here so soon."

"I'm only staying till to-morrow morning," Mr. Prentice replied. "I have just had a look at the lie of the land and heard all the details of the dispute from your father."

Toddy looked at him keenly for the first time since he had come into the room.

"Well, I should sit down if I were you; it seems to have shaken you a bit," he said.

Mr. Prentice sat down without protest.

"Yes," Toddy went on, "you seem to have made a hit with Violette. As a rule, she's inclined to be somewhat short with people; but people, of course, have a way of being rather rude to her. Iris wasn't too clever; still, I owe her the introduction, so I'll leave my sister out of it."

"Introduction?" Mr. Prentice repeated, as if he hadn't heard the word correctly.

"My sister had an extraordinary effect on the kid, you know," Toddy said, "and Violette became rather fed up with it all. I don't think really it was Iris's fault; she was just a magnet. She's always had the same attraction for most men, you know; must be damned irritating for her because I don't think she really likes anyone very much. She's sufficient to herself, if you know what I mean. Violette came over in a tearing rage one day and I happened to be there and tried to make the peace." He laughed. "I made it so well that Iris won't speak to me."

"Mrs. Dawson is a very nice woman," Mr. Prentice said with enthusiasm.

Toddy raised his eyebrows and looked at him with some surprise.

"I should hardly call her that," he replied, and Mr. Prentice remembered that Mr. Speed had raised a similar objection to the word "nice". "But at heart she's a very good sort and she's shed what she calls her illusions. By the way, she doesn't appear to think you've shed yours, and she thinks you're rather sweet; whatever that means."

"Very kind of her," Mr. Prentice put in, beaming all over his face which had now regained most of its former colour.

"Of course, she'd leave me to-morrow if she felt like it," Toddy went on airily, "but as I'd do the same to her there's no harm done."

Mr. Prentice looked a little shocked.

"I think——" he began.

"I know what you think, but you're getting on a bit," Toddy interrupted him. "I've read a little, you know; and anyway, after the last war, let alone the one before, you can't expect young people to cling to much in the way of ideals. No, everlasting love is a myth. So is everything else." He paused. "I can't express exactly what I mean, but nothing means anything any more. You have one obligation, pay as you earn, and that applies, and nothing else, to everything. In my case it's better to have a friendship with a little fun thrown in than a lot of fun with no friendship, or a friendship without any fun at all. I regard my sister, for instance, as a perfectly useless individual."

"Lady Iris! Why?" Mr. Prentice asked, his cogent arguments which he had been marshalling to squash the materialistic young man flying out of the window at the sudden mention of his sister's name.

"She just causes trouble, and she has no intention of doing anything about it," he explained.

"But you've just said you didn't think it was her fault," Mr. Prentice expostulated.

"Perhaps it isn't in one sense," Toddy replied, "but it is her fault that she doesn't give way to someone's charms.

The world can't be stocked entirely with pike; I mean, there must be an attractive fish somewhere. Yet Iris has never looked like taking any serious notice of anyone; the men become serious and then there's hell to pay and Iris tosses those dark curls of hers and puts on what I call her virginal smirk and another poor devil has had it, but not her. She's blown up that ruddy courtyard, Violette tells me; though I had a fair idea what was happening before Violette got venomous and let fly." He felt in his pocket for his cigarette case and lit a cigarette. "Not that I care a damn about the Fawcetts, the Speeds and the Cummings of this world; Iris is worth more than all of them put together. There're plenty of them; they are ordinary people, like I am, but Iris—she's different."

Mr. Prentice leaned forward and cocked his right ear nearer to the speaker to hear him better.

"In what way?" he asked.

"In every way," Toddy replied. "She's a very talented person and she's a very travelled woman. Heaven alone knows what mischief she's made abroad, but there are very few places of any importance that Iris hasn't managed to visit."

Mr. Prentice leaned back again in his chair. He didn't know what answer he had expected her brother to give him, but he was conscious of a feeling of acute disappointment; and yet there was nothing at which to cavil in the reply. Only Mr. Prentice already knew that she was a great traveller, that as he understood matters was inevitable. He leaned forward again and fired another question, more important he felt to him that the last.

"And where is she now?" he asked.

Toddy shrugged his shoulders.

"Heaven alone knows! I don't and, by the look of the letters in the hall, the old man doesn't either," Toddy answered. "She has a way of running off by herself and sending picture postcards."

"She's been away some time this time without sending any word," Mr. Prentice commented.

Toddy frowned and appeared a little disturbed.

"I suppose she has," he admitted rather grudgingly.

"Yes, now that I come to think of it, I suppose she has." As the library door opened he shot a warning glance at Mr. Prentice, laid his fingers on his lips and shook his head. "Not in front of father," he whispered. Lord Rawton came into the room on the death of the sound and Toddy rose quietly to his feet.

"I see you've got Mr. Prentice down already," he said. "You don't let the grass grow long, do you?"

His father gave him a smile.

"I didn't know you were coming down, Toddy," he said. "Mr. Prentice and I have finished our business. Have you seen old Tonks and told him you are here?"

Toddy nodded.

"I've also told him to open a bottle of decent port," he said. "I don't know why, but I never knew a barrister who didn't like port."

"Quite right," his father answered, sitting down. "Where have you been, Mr. Prentice?"

Mr. Prentice hesitated a moment.

"I made for the Rawton Arms," he said, "and incidentally had a chat with Mrs. Huggins," he added with a side glance at Toddy. Though the latter showed no sign of interest Lord Rawton frowned as if he found the subject a little bewildering and then turned to his son.

"That reminds me," he said, "where is Iris? I wish you'd readdress her letters while you're here. She's never troubled to tell me where she is, so I can't do anything about them."

Toddy, after a start of surprise occasioned, Mr. Prentice surmised, by his father's unexpected show of interest in his daughter, shrugged his shoulders.

"I don't know any more than you do," he admitted. "Mr. Prentice has, as a matter of fact, just reminded me that she's been away some time without, apparently, telling anyone." His frank, good-humoured face set in troubled lines once again. "I suppose she's all right," he added doubtfully.

"Of course she is," his father snapped back at him, but with all the certainty of his reply Mr. Prentice saw his grave eyes waver, and his long frame stirred uneasily in his chair

F

"When did you see or hear from her last?" he asked after a moment.

"I've been in her house about a week," Mr. Prentice put in helpfully. "I don't know, of course, how long the house was left empty before I took possession."

Toddy screwed up his eyes while he made a calculation.

"It must have been nearly three weeks to a month since I saw her," he said at length. "But then we had——" he stopped abruptly. "She put all her stuff in store. I imagined she was coming back here," he added.

His father shook his head impatiently as if he thought his son's idea a very stupid one, but he made no other answer and from his abstraction Mr. Prentice guessed that his mind had strayed from the immediate present and that, though he was still thinking of his daughter, it was of other times and circumstances.

"Of course, she's done this before," Toddy began.

"Frequently," his father interrupted him dryly. "But someone generally knew where she was, or she let someone know pretty soon. I've never been able to make head or tail of her." He paused and his mouth quivered. "But perhaps that's not surprising," he muttered to himself.

"I don't know whether it's of any interest or help to you," Mr. Prentice put in diffidently, "but I do happen to know that at least two people, and perhaps three, have been trying to get in touch with her during the last week or two. One person in particular—he has not been successful."

"Getting in touch with her? What for?" Lord Rawton asked.

Mr. Prentice looked at Toddy, but his expression was neither helpful nor deterring and Mr. Prentice, who had opened the vein he had decided a little while ago to ignore, found himself at a loss. It was no good, he felt, trying to explain the pattern to Lord Rawton or his son, at least certainly not the mysterious centre of it, and any explanation of the border made him a common informer—a rôle for which he had no stomach.

"I think they were worried," he temporized. "In fact, I am sure they were. I mean, if someone who has lived next door for over a year suddenly moves their caravan overnight, as it were, and none of her friends knows what has happened to her; she has not come back, she is not in her usual haunts and there is no word from her, naturally anyone with any humanity would be worried." In spite of his hasty and ungrammatical marshalling of his facts Mr. Prentice had no trouble in making himself understood.

"Although you've never met Iris you appear to know a great deal about her affairs," Lord Rawton replied.

Mr. Prentice, at first, thought her father was being resentful, but on looking at him he found that he was merely curious.

"I must say," Toddy suddenly broke in, "I didn't realize— I wonder if we ought——"

"Iris has always managed her own life in her own way," his father interrupted him sharply, "and, except that her own management has always led to trouble for someone, it has been very successful from her own point of view. I'm not going to be stampeded into anything only to be told by Iris that I am an idiot who can't mind his own business. If she was in trouble we should have heard soon enough."

Toddy did not appear, Mr. Prentice thought, to be much heartened by his father's remarks, but whether he was or not they were interrupted by Tonks who announced dinner.

"I'm afraid," Lord Rawton said to Mr. Prentice as they moved towards the hall, "you'll have to put up with us as we are. I have three children, but only two indoor servants," he explained. "Tonks and his wife. She is an indifferent cook and he is an indifferent butler."

Mr. Prentice noticed that throughout the rest of the evening Lord Rawton was prepared to talk about any subject except that of his daughter, and that his son, though he kept the ball of conversation moving, was by no means the self-possessed young man whom he had discovered on his return from his walk. But whether it was the vintage port, or the generous measure of whisky which Toddy subsequently poured out for him, or the shaking of his senses down by the reeds in the mere had left stronger tremors behind than he had thought, Mr. Prentice began to feel light-headed and very sleepy, and the desultory conversation carried on between the father and the son sounded less and less coherent.

He caught Toddy looking at him a little curiously and, surprising what was little better than a smirk upon his face, rose to his feet with resolution. To his astonishment he appeared to be standing rather quicker than he had anticipated, and his balance was temporarily unsteady. However, he gave Lord Rawton, and his son a very warm and friendly smile and announced with great good humour that he thought he had better be going to bed as he had had a long day. Having made his decision he did not hesitate, but went towards the door without further ado, and was gratified to find that Toddy had anticipated his wishes by getting there first and opening it for him.

"I'll come up with you and see you're comfortable," he offered.

"There's no need at all," Mr. Prentice answered genially. "Not the slightest—I assure you. I can manage perfectly well. I know exactly where I am."

With which he advanced with commendable accuracy and speed towards the grand staircase and, mounting the marble stairs one by one, had a curious feeling that perhaps, when he reached the top, the wall in front of him would open and he would find a similar flight descending on the other side. But the wall remained in place and, turning to the left, he was lost to Toddy's sight as he made his way towards the bathroom and his own room.

Reaching his room he switched on the light and, without looking to the right or the left of him, picked up his spongebag and razor case from the marble table and went into the bathroom. Returning later he shut the door behind him and, still keeping his eyes lowered, tumbled himself out of his clothes and into his pair of striped pyjamas, the tying of the strings of which appeared to him to be a matter of very considerable difficulty. But it was accomplished at length and he stood by the bed from which the golden counterpane had been removed, looking owlishly at the torch lights that flanked it. But try as he would to keep his eyes upon them and the switch which he saw regulated them, he felt an irrepressible desire to turn his head and, having turned it, saw that not only was Iris smiling at him, but that her picture was softly lit. The quality of the smile had not altered and Mr. Prentice tried to drive himself to combat its complacent superiority.

"No," he muttered to himself, averting his eyes hastily, "not I."

Knowing not where to look to avoid the eyes of Iris and the image of her in her samite gown with her staff and golden wings, he looked upward, and his eyes became fixed upon that star in the vaulted roof which was brighter than the rest. Immediately he experienced an extreme dizziness. There was a throbbing in his head, a weakness in his knees and an uncertainty in his vision. The ceiling appeared to move, then falter, then move again; the golden curtains stirred restlessly and Mr. Prentice felt his senses leaving him and, as he fell upon the bed, there rolled about him "the surge and thunder of the Odyssey".

In the morning he found himself in his bed; he had no idea when he had got into it, but the lights still shone, palely protesting against the morning sun. After one horrified glance at them he turned them off and, blinking about him and moving his rough tongue about his dry mouth, he gazed upward at the ceiling without emotion. Greatly daring he darted a look at Iris, but though she still smiled he could detect no malice. He felt utterly spent and without vitality, but there was a restfulness in the room which he had not recognized before. Unexpectedly he found himself lapped in security and no longer fretted either with the secret of the pattern or with the ordinary problems of life. He suddenly knew without any possible doubt that there was nothing more to be done but to wait for the culmination; he had suspected something earlier, but nothing so grave.

No man can avert a thunderstorm; it rides its black horse from the edge of the horizon and man can only stand still. With certainty comes peace of mind. Had he only been able to repeat the aphorism on the previous night, Mr. Prentice knew that he would not have tried to stifle his forebodings in the folds of Bacchus's gown.

In the morning one is apt to be honest with oneself and

Mr. Prentice admitted that his lapse from sobriety was, indeed, no accident; he had wanted to smother his senses because he had heard what others had not; because he had seen what others had not; and too late he had wanted to deaden the sound and to blow out the light. But now, when he realized that the fight was over and knew that nothing could delay the inevitable end, he had the courage of the vanquished who had nothing left to them but honour. Rising slowly from his low bed with the golden scrolls, he stood in his ridiculous striped pyjamas in front of Iris. But the smile mocked him still.

"You slept well?" Lord Rawton asked him at the breakfast table.

Mr. Prentice could detect no note of irony in the enquiry. "Thank you, yes," he answered.

"I'm glad of that," Lord Rawton said. "Some people don't. They find the room rather strange and they feel restless. Toddy will drive you to the station; I gather he's going up to London as well."

It was in the car that Toddy made his only reference to his sister.

"You worried me last night," he admitted. "Do you think that anything is really wrong? I mean, do you think anything can have happened to Iris? I'd no idea no one had heard from her."

Mr. Prentice stirred uneasily.

"I think," he said quietly after a little pause, "that no one will hear from Iris again."

Toddy pursed his lips, glanced swiftly at Mr. Prentice and as swiftly looked away.

"Nonsense," he answered.

Mr. Prentice did not contradict him.

The train was so full that Mr. Prentice and Toddy gave up all attempts at conversation, but he could see that his companion was thinking out a problem to himself. What it was he didn't know, but by the abrupt way in which Toddy accepted his thanks, bade him good-bye and walked away, Mr. Prentice surmised that he had made a decision and was already in the process of implementing it.

Mr. Prentice had hardly made his way back to his house, after calling in at his chambers, when he and Markham were interrupted by the ringing of the door bell. Markham went across to the study window and, peeping through the curtains, gave a sigh.

"There he is again," he said.

"Who?" Mr. Prentice asked.

"That Fawcett fellow," Markham replied. "He looked in this morning to see you and, when I told him you'd gone to Rawton Hall, he started as if he'd been stung by a bee and said he'd be back. This is his third attempt."

"Well, you'd better let him in, I suppose," Mr. Prentice said.

Mr. Fawcett swept into the room like a ship before the wind and his thin figure of foreboding looked more tenuous than ever. His eyes were rimmed red with lack of sleep and the veins stood knotted and blue on the backs of his trembling hands. Hardly waiting for Markham to close the door he rushed towards Mr. Prentice, his neck thrust out and his hands wavering in front of him like those of a blind man seeking support.

"You've found her?" he gasped.

Mr. Prentice looked at him coldly.

"If you mean Lady Iris," he replied, "she was not at the Hall."

"But her father knew where she was," Mr. Fawcett said eagerly.

Mr. Prentice shook his head.

"He did not," he answered, "nor, so far as I know, does anyone else."

Mr. Fawcett appeared to take a long time to master the exact terms of the reply; then he collapsed, rather than sat, on the nearest chair and stared in front of him like a man bereft of half his senses and all hope. In spite of his antagonism towards himself Mr. Prentice felt a pang of sorrow for him.

"I think," he said gently, "that it may not be a long time now before she is found."

"It will be too late," Mr. Fawcett answered wildly. "Too late; and I shall have killed her." He looked up with his wild and gummy eyes. "D'you hear?" he went on. "Are you listening? I shall have killed her."

Mr. Prentice, whose old horror of scenes, even in the Law Courts, oppressed him, patted him soothingly on the shoulder.

"Nothing is gained," he said sententiously, "by losing control of yourself. Let us try and face the matter calmly. Why are you so sure that she is dead and what has it got to do with you?"

Whether it was due to Mr. Prentice's actions or because he was exhausted, Mr. Fawcett stared dully in front of him and the fire left his veins; his lips moved, but no sound came.

"I think I understand how it is," Mr. Prentice put in after a little while. "You saw that she was breaking up the life of the nice couple next door and you went to see her to give her a piece of advice. She didn't take it because she said it was no business of hers; but Norman Cumming kept on going round and you stayed. You threatened her with hell fire and she laughed at you."

"Yes, she laughed," Mr. Fawcett muttered. " 'But, behold the day cometh' " he cried, " 'that shall burn as an oven; and all the proud, yea, and all that do wickedly, shall be stubble; and the day that cometh shall burn them up, saith the Lord of Hosts, that it shall leave them neither root nor branch. But unto you that fear My Name shall the Sun of Righteousness arise with healing in his wings.' " His voice sank to a whisper again and Mr. Prentice laid his hand once more upon his shoulder.

"But she would not listen," Mr. Prentice said, and then he repeated more fully what he had said to Norman Cumming. "She is neither Christian, nor Mahommedan nor Jew. She is pagan."

Mr. Fawcett raised himself from his stupor.

"I don't know how you know," he admitted, "but you are right. She is not like anyone else; there is a severity about her and a mischievous knowledge. She let me talk, but she paid no attention until one day she suddenly put her hands to her ears and said she had had enough. She told me that I had won, that I was right and that she was going. 'It is your world' she said, 'and I have been too long in it. It is many years now since I came; I should have gone back before this. There was a message I had to give. I shouldn't have delayed so long.' I didn't know what she meant, but suddenly one evening I found this house bare and she had gone. Now I know that what she said could only have meant one thing. I have tried to prevent it, but I feel that I have not succeeded and shall not succeed.''

Mr. Prentice listened to him, but he did not pay much attention to what he was actually saying. His imagination was adrift on perilous seas and the centre of the pattern took surer shape, but he did not enlighten Mr. Fawcett. Instead, he walked away from him and addressed him in a matter-of-fact tone of voice.

"It is a pity," he said, "that you should have been so hostile with her. After all, they ran after her, you know, and not she after them. And she didn't disappear from here because she was afraid of hell fire and she didn't leave because of anything you threatened."

Mr. Fawcett started up eagerly at his confidence and his face became transformed with a glow almost of happiness.

"Then you don't think it is because of anything I threatened?" he began.

"No," Mr. Prentice interrupted him quietly. "I don't. It is because of something that you did."

"I did?" Mr. Fawcett repeated without understanding.

"You've omitted to tell me," Mr. Prentice went on inexorably, "that you fell in love with her yourself. That was why she stopped her ears. You were the apostle of the new truth; the fiery prophet of the new world—a world and a truth, that is to say, that were new to her. But she found ugliness and deceit even in you. The Gods gave you and me a world of beauty and what have we done with it? There are some people, you know, who think that the words attributed to Julian have a melancholy significance to-day."

"What words?" Mr. Fawcett asked.

"'Thou hast conquered, O Galilean,'" Mr. Prentice answered.

"I don't know them: I don't understand them," Mr. Fawcett muttered.

"That's just the trouble," Mr. Prentice replied gently. "Very few people understand anything and their number is getting less. It is all very well to look out of your window and see the mechanical marvels of man and say that is progress, but I don't have to tell you that what one's eyes see is of small account beside what is hidden from them. Anyone can find out, or some intelligent child will tell them, that the rainbow, for instance, consists of concentric and circular arcs, that its angular radius is between 40 and 41 degrees, and its colours are those of the spectrum. You can also write a geometrical treatise on it if you have a mind to do so. But," he paused, "that isn't the end of it, you know."

"What is the end of it?" Mr. Fawcett asked.

"The next time you see one," Mr. Prentice advised him, "try if you can to find out. But as a starting point suppose you begin a search for beauty; and when you have found the smallest particle of it, cling to it and don't let it escape you. It is the bridge between peoples and the bridge between heaven and earth. It is——"

Mr. Prentice was stopped in full flight by Markham who came in a little apologetically.

"I'm sorry to interrupt," he said, giving the forlorn figure of Mr. Fawcett a curious glance, "but there's a Mr. Treacher outside and he said he'd like to see you at once. I told him you were engaged and he said he'd wait. I told him he couldn't do that. He said, oh yes, he could. Quite determined; then he said he was Scotland Yard and I said that was different."

The mention of Scotland Yard had an immediate effect on Mr. Fawcett who nearly recovered his equilibrium at one bound, and felt again very much in the ascendant as he gave Mr. Prentice a glance that dubbed him then and there a criminal.

"I'll be going," he said hurriedly and, without waiting, left the room with his curious raking stride. Mr. Prentice watched him go and shrugged his shoulders. The lesson had not been learnt, he knew that.

"Well, show him in," he said impatiently, "and don't listen at the door. I haven't stolen anything, nor have I done anything else to bring me within the grasp of the law."

Markham showed Mr. Treacher in and Mr. Prentice raised his eyebrows at the clean-shaven and sharp-nosed young man who apologized at once for his intrusion.

"Yes?" Mr. Prentice murmured politely.

"I find myself in a somewhat difficult position," Mr. Treacher began. "In fact I am rather at a loss to justify my intrusion." He gave Mr. Prentice a diffident smile. "But as you appear to be responsible for this odd state of affairs in some way——"

"I!" Mr. Prentice exclaimed, indicating a chair with a wave of his pudgy hand, but the young detective, still smiling, refused it.

"I'd rather stand, thank you," he went on. "So far as I can make out," he continued with more confidence, "in consequence of something you said to Mr. Todhunter he came down to the Yard. He appears to be worried because he has heard nothing of his sister for some time."

"Quite," replied Mr. Prentice who could think of nothing else to say.

"I gather that his father is not prepared at the moment to take any active measures and that makes his own position somewhat difficult," Mr. Treacher went on. "He wants us, apparently, to do what we can without starting a hue and cry. But, as I think the chief told him, we can't really be expected to chase will-o'-the-wisps all over the country. Of course, there is a difference between Lord Rawton's daughter and any stray woman who disappears; but even so, unless he is prepared to put the matter officially in our hands so that we can advise the press, if we think fit and so forth, things are apt to be pretty nebulous."

"I can appreciate that," Mr. Prentice answered.

"However," Mr. Treacher went on, "it so happened that I was hanging about when Mr. Todhunter came in, and when he gave Lady Iris's last address, which was this house, the chief apparently changed his mind. I mean he was about to throw him out on his ear, so to speak."

"What has this house got to do with it?" Mr. Prentice asked.

"Because I happen to live at Number 2," Mr. Treacher said, "and therefore am, so to speak, on the spot."

"That makes it all very tidy," Mr. Prentice murmured to himself. "In fact it completes the border."

He looked at the young man with greater interest while the latter looked very puzzled at the interjection.

"I know you all by sight," Mr. Treacher went on pleasantly after a moment, "and one by sound as well as by sight— that child opposite. Apart from yourself, Mr. Todhunter suggested the other people living here as possible avenues for enquiry. As a matter of fact, I have had a word with all of them except you and Mr. Fawcett."

"You have?" Mr. Prentice said. "I suppose you wouldn't care to tell me what they said," he went on.

The young detective shrugged his shoulders.

"Certainly," he answered. "It won't take a moment. They said virtually nothing."

"Nothing?" Mr. Prentice exclaimed.

"You seem surprised," Mr. Treacher said. "I can't say I was. I gather that they none of them knew Lady Iris very well; they one and all told me that they saw no reason why they should have been told where she was going. London is quite different from the country or even from the suburbs."

"Quite," Mr. Prentice put in dryly. "You saw both Mr. and Mrs. Cumming?" he went on in surprised tones.

"Why not?"

"They went away," Mr. Prentice replied carefully. "I'd no idea they were both back."

"That's just the point I'm making about Lady Iris," the young detective said, "and the one they made to me. You don't know the comings and goings of your neighbours and why should you? Although——" he paused and a small, worried frown creased his forehead.

"Although——" Mr. Prentice prompted him.

"Well, they did seem to be concealing something," he went on. "I suppose you've no idea what that might be?"

Mr. Prentice shook his head slowly.

"I can't be expected to guess what's at the back of the minds of other people," he answered.

"Of course not," Mr. Treacher agreed. "Well, sir," he continued, "now to come to you. I gathered from Mr. Todhunter that it was your anxiety over Lady Iris's apparent silence that really upset him. What help can you give me?"

Mr. Prentice looked at the detective a little uncomfortably.

"I've never even met Lady Iris," he said.

"Never met her!" Mr. Treacher exclaimed.

"Not in the flesh," Mr. Prentice replied. Then he raised his mild eyes and meeting the detective's incredulous stare, blinked. "Though one night last week," he went on diffidently, "I thought I saw her, but it was only a dream, you know."

Mr. Treacher continued to give him a searching glance as if he doubted his sanity, and was engaged in having a good look for it.

"But," he said at length, "what have you got to go on? I mean, why do you think something's happened to her? In fact, I gathered from Mr. Todhunter that you were certain."

Mr. Prentice continued to look very uncomfortable as the young detective waited expectantly for something more cogent. After an awkward silence Mr. Prentice did speak again, but not in the strain Mr. Treacher hoped or expected.

"There's a poem of Kipling's," he began hurriedly. "You probably know it. A bit of it goes like this:

'O this I have felt, and this I have guessed and this I
    have heard men say
  And this a man wrote that another man wrote of an Earl
    in Norroway.
  Ye have read, ye have felt, ye have guessed, good lack!
    ye have hampered heaven's gate;
  There's little room between the stars of idleness to prate.'

You follow me?"

Mr. Treacher scratched his head.

"You mean you have no facts," he answered at length.

Mr. Prentice's sunny smile chased the indeterminate expression from his face.

"Exactly," he replied. "I've no facts to give you except negative ones. I don't know Lady Iris; I don't know where she went and I don't know where she is."

"Then, if I may say so, sir," Mr. Treacher said sharply, "it seems a pity that you should have expressed yourself with such certainty to Mr. Todhunter." He turned towards the door abruptly. "I'll have a word with Mr. Fawcett, but I don't expect he'll be any more helpful than the rest of you."

"I'm sorry if——" Mr. Prentice began. "I shouldn't like you to think," he started again, "that what I said was just empty talk. But I do know that the police are concerned with facts, not fantasies. I can give you none."

Mr. Treacher turned again.

"You can't suggest any place she might be likely to be?" he asked.

"I can suggest a great many," Mr. Prentice answered, "but the suggestions wouldn't avail you much. There are many lonely pastoral places in the British Isles, and in one of them I think she will be found."

Mr. Treacher shrugged his shoulders.

"That's not very helpful," he remarked. "If you are so certain that there is going to be a tragedy," he continued with a touch of asperity, "you don't appear to want to prevent it much."

"My dear young man," Mr. Prentice replied with great gentleness, "you misunderstand me. I can't do anything about it. I am resigned to the inevitable, and when one is that there is no reason to rend one's garments or rush about the world like an idle wind. But I am sadder than anyone else about it."

"And yet you've never met her!" Mr. Treacher exclaimed sarcastically. "It seems to me that all this is so much waste of my time." He shrugged his shoulders. "However, I'll have a word with Mr. Fawcett."

"I very much doubt if he'll give you anything except a sharp dose of what he labels Christianity," Mr. Prentice replied.

The detective gave him a last look of mingled curiosity and irritation.

"Probably not," he replied. "None of you seem to want to be accommodating. I have a feeling I am not being told the facts, but perhaps that's only because there aren't any."

He waited for Mr. Prentice to say something in answer, but when he did nothing but look at him uncomfortably, he turned to the door again and left the study, taking with him a very muddled picture of Mr. Prentice, but oddly enough a very clear one of Miss Lottie Spate whose photograph on the mantelpiece appeared to him to be as much out of keeping with the room as Mr. Prentice seemed out of touch with reality.

He had hardly taken his leave when the bell in Mr. Prentice's house was rung again and, as Mr. Prentice happened to be standing in his hall at the time looking undecided and ill at ease, he opened the door himself to find Joyce Cumming, rather pale and by no means so certain of herself as usual, standing in the doorway. She slid past him and into the study before Mr. Prentice had time to give her a word of greeting. Motioning him to shut the door, she looked at him with a pair of frightened eyes, while her fingers pulled restlessly at her tiny handkerchief which was rolled up in a ball in her hands.

"Has that detective been here?" she asked. "Of course he has," she went on breathlessly. "I've been waiting for him to go."

Mr. Prentice put his squat hand on her thin shoulder and gave her a reassuring pat.

"What did he want?" she went on. "It was about Iris, wasn't it?"

Mr. Prentice nodded and Joyce threw her head back with a touch of defiance.

"We're in one hell of a mess," she said. "At least, I am." She sat down suddenly and stared in front of her. "I never thought——" she began. "If——"

"Can I help at all?" Mr. Prentice asked.

"That's what I came here for," Joyce replied candidly. "You're a barrister; I want some advice."

Mr. Prentice looked at her a little sadly.

"I had hoped when Mr. Treacher told me that you and your husband were back that——"

"Oh, it's nothing to do with us," Joyce interrupted him. "I mean, we have kissed and are friends and all that. It's the revolver."

"Revolver?" Mr. Prentice repeated a little vaguely.

"I thought I had hidden it so carefully," Joyce went on. "I told you so, you remember?" Mr. Prentice nodded. "Then suddenly I became afraid. Norman was so—so—unbalanced: and so I rushed up here yesterday; and it wasn't where I had put it. And I thought Norman must have got hold of it. I was nearly frantic. I thought, you see——"

"I understand," Mr. Prentice put in gently.

"Then, of course, there was a hopeless anticlimax because I got hold of him at the office." Joyce laughed a little hysterically. "He came along here at once and, at last, we had the lid off, if you know what I mean. We'd never really come to grips before and we forgot everything else for a little." She looked at him a little more calmly. "But the revolver has gone; and so has Iris." Mr. Prentice nodded to her. "She knew I had it; and she could have taken it. Norman has told me she was in the house with him. That was unlike her. He used to come and see her, but she never came to see him. She asked him to go round for her to one of the shops for some wretched thing or another. You see——" she spread out her hands.

"You didn't tell Mr. Treacher," Mr. Prentice said.

Joyce shook her head decidedly.

"No, we didn't. After all I may be wrong," she went on half-heartedly, and Mr. Prentice knew that she didn't believe she was. "We can't do anything, can we? And we want to keep out of it. That's why I came round to see you. Norman didn't want me to, but somehow I thought you'd be a help."

"But if you are right," Mr. Prentice answered, "when the police find Lady Iris they will also find the revolver, and they will trace the ownership without much trouble. Your husband must know that. Presumably he has a licence."

Joyce shook her head.

"He hasn't; it's a Hun revolver," she said. "He brought it back with him. That's why we thought we might— do you think it makes any difference whether we tell or not?"

"No," Mr. Prentice replied slowly. "I don't think it makes any difference. Though I am quite sure that Mr. Treacher would think that it did."

"But it wouldn't, would it?" Joyce pressed him and Mr. Prentice slowly gave again what she hoped he would, a deliberate and negative shake of the head. Joyce smoothed her dress with nervous hands and rose to her feet precipitately.

"Well, that's that," she said, giving him a fleeting pale smile. "We may be wrong, after all. Norman is afraid that——" she stopped abruptly.

"Afraid of what?"

"Well, I threatened her, and he thinks perhaps she might——"

Mr. Prentice shook his head again.

"I think the Gods have punished him sufficiently," he put in enigmatically. "It isn't for mortals to fall in love with goddesses. Remember Ixion."

Joyce gave him a bewildered stare and Mr. Prentice once more laid his hand upon her shoulder and, pushing her gently before him, escorted her out of the house into the courtyard where Mr. Speed was standing at his front door pretending to look at the heavens. At the appearance of Mr. Prentice, however, he gave up his pretence and, the moment Joyce had waved a perfunctory farewell, beckoned across the courtyard to him.

"Come along in," he said. "I'd like a word with you."

As Mr. Prentice waddled rather than walked towards him, he watched his progress with a faint gleam of amusement in his muddy green eyes. "We're having quite a conversation piece here one way and another," he continued. "People popping in and out of each other's houses—just like a French farce. I hear you've been up to the Hall." He inclined his great back slightly and allowed Mr. Prentice to get past him. "Have you had a visit from that detective chap? Funny thing he should live at Number 2. Have a glass of something? I'm on the wagon for a bit. I've given up dying by noggins—it was upsetting my judgment. Did some pretty foolish things the last week or so. Better now."

Mr. Prentice looked at him curiously.

"You've got over your—I mean—you don't——" he began.

"If you mean am I still worrying my heart and soul over Iris, I'm not," Mr. Speed interrupted him. "I'm worried, yes: but the magic's gone. You didn't get any news of her?" He gave Mr. Prentice a keen glance.

"No," he said, "I didn't."

"I gather her brother's got the wind up," Mr. Speed said. "A bit late in the day, I shouldn't wonder. Though you never know with women, do you? That detective fellow asked me a lot of damn fool questions." He shrugged his shoulders. "I knew nothing and, if I had, I wouldn't have told him. I don't want to have anything to do with the police."

"So the magic's gone out," Mr. Prentice repeated to himself thoughtfully. "It appears to have died across the way as well." He looked at Mr. Speed shyly. "You've been away too?" he went on tentatively.

"Yes," Mr. Speed snapped back. "I was an ass. I told myself I wouldn't go and then I had a hunch, or thought I had. I drew a blank. Then when I was alone, miles from anywhere, I suddenly decided to let go, as it were. I have let go and, if Iris came past my window on the tips of her toes, I shouldn't——" he stopped.

"You wouldn't what?" Mr. Prentice prompted him.

"I wouldn't look up," Mr. Speed went on doggedly. "No, sir. When I let go, I let go. Cut my losses and start again. And oddly enough it wasn't so difficult and it's getting easier." He glanced at Mr. Prentice sharply. "I expect you're laughing at me, saying to yourself what an exhibition! How soon love blows! But it wasn't love; it was something more powerful than that, but the power is dying."

"Yes, the power is dying," Mr. Prentice repeated.

"I don't quite understand now how I could have——" Mr. Speed began and his great brow became furrowed, and he shook his head a little helplessly. "It was so unlike me;

but there was something there. Yes, there was something there. But what it was I don't know. I thought I did at one time, but it escaped me."

"Like the trailing cloak," Mr. Prentice said.

"You don't think she'll come back, do you?" Mr. Speed asked him suddenly.

"I don't," Mr. Prentice answered confidently and he heard Mr. Speed's great sigh—whether of relief or sorrow he wasn't certain.

"You think she's dead," he said after a moment. "You said as much to Todhunter, so that detective fellow told me. Why do you think she committed suicide? Or do you think someone's killed her?"

"I don't think she's dead yet," Mr. Prentice replied gently. "But I think she will die, and that very soon."

Mr. Speed looked at him curiously.

"You're an odd little beast," he said and, becoming aware that the light in the room had gradually deteriorated so that even the modern furniture and embellishments looked dull and indistinct, he shook himself like a dog as if to loose the load of apprehension from his broad shoulders.

"It's got damned dark!" he exclaimed, striding towards the window. "There's a devil of a storm coming."

Pulling back the curtains, he looked out and upwards and saw the feathery leaves of the ash threshing in the wind against the sable sky. But Mr. Prentice did not follow him; instead he remained standing in the middle of the room and his chubby face grew a little paler, and his short little hands were bunched together. He had the air of a man who had braced himself to accept the inevitable and was waiting patiently for the fatal fulfilment.

"One hell of a storm," Mr. Speed muttered uneasily and, as he spoke, there came one shattering clap of thunder and the heavens opened to deluge the courtyard. Mr. Prentice slowly relaxed and, as he listened to the rain, his mind came suddenly to rest.

"It won't last long." He heard a voice and knew it was his own replying to Mr. Speed and found himself moving over to the window, but when he reached it he found that his view was too restricted, and he hurried away to the front door which he flung open in spite of Mr. Speed's protest against letting the rain into his hall. There he stood, watching the heavens through the tossing leaves of the tree, and saw the rain stop as suddenly as it had begun. He watched the sun blaze again; he saw the leaves lie peaceful and, above the topmost branches across the blue sky, caught a glimpse of what he had come out to see—the rainbow; and he gave it a smile, a sad and friendly smile.

"So you don't think she's dead." Mr. Speed's voice sounded behind him.

Mr. Prentice stepped into the wet courtyard.

"Oh, but I do," he said and, walking away towards his own house, left Mr. Speed staring after him.

It was much later in the evening, a little before his dinner time, in fact, when Mr. Prentice was disturbed again, and it was by Mr. Treacher whose sharp features seemed to Mr. Prentice to look bleaker than they had done previously. He stood in the middle of his study, his homburg in his hand, while Lottie Spate sniffed at his heels suspiciously.

"I am sorry to disturb you again, Mr. Prentice," he began.

"Not at all," replied Mr. Prentice, "I am glad to see you." He cocked an eye at him. "By the way, how did you get on with Mr. Fawcett?"

"About as well as I did with the rest of you," the young detective admitted. "In other words I didn't get on at all. There is either a conspiracy of silence, or none of her neighbours really knows anything."

"You were one of her neighbours yourself," Mr. Prentice reminded him.

Mr. Treacher nodded.

"I don't think I ever saw the lady," he said. "I am not about here much in the daytime as a rule. However, I didn't disturb you to waste your time; the fact is I have just been telephoned to by the Yard who have themselves just been rung up. A young woman, believed to be Lady Iris, has been found dead." He looked at Mr. Prentice speculatively. "I was wondering whether you would like to tell me anything you may know now that she's been found. You were so certain she was not alive, weren't you? Would you care now to tell me why?"

Mr. Prentice hesitated.

"My dear Mr. Treacher," he replied at length, "surely it is only common sense. Lady Iris was hardly a woman who could disappear for a number of weeks without leaving any trace whatsoever. I don't think that her brother, for instance, had any idea that no one at all had heard anything of her. He only knew that he hadn't."

Mr. Treacher smiled at him a little incredulously.

"Surely you had more to go on than that," he suggested.

"Nothing more that would help you," Mr. Prentice said. "In any case, why should you worry your head about it? If a person shoots herself—or drowns herself," he added hastily, but not before Mr. Treacher had given him a sharp look, "it may be a tragedy that it wasn't prevented, but——" he paused. "How did she—die, as a matter of fact?"

Mr. Treacher did not reply at once; then he suddenly made up his mind.

"She was shot. It looks like suicide. The revolver——" Mr. Treacher paused in his reply, "the revolver," he repeated, "is of German make."

"Ah!" exclaimed Mr. Prentice.

"What I am trying to find out is where she got it from; and I also want any light anyone can throw on the state of her mind at the time she went away. I have, of course, seen everyone again this evening—I mean all the people here— they all say that the last time they saw her she was quite normal. Mr. Fawcett, however, volunteered a slightly in- coherent opinion based on the assumption that the wages of sin is death."

"What sin did Mr. Fawcett think she had committed?" Mr. Prentice asked.

"I gather he regarded her beauty as a sin," Mr. Treacher answered dryly.

"We could do with more sin, if that is so," Mr. Prentice retorted. "That is the trouble with the world to-day. It has grown very ugly."

"Perhaps, but whether it is beautiful or ugly doesn't help

me at all," Mr. Treacher said. "Why did Lady Iris leave here so suddenly? Tell me that."

"The neighbours might know," Mr. Prentice replied.

"If they do, they won't say."

"It's no use asking me," Mr. Prentice said. "I've already told you I've never met the lady."

Mr. Treacher looked at him a moment and then shrugged his shoulders.

"If you won't help, you won't," he said, and turning on his heel went quickly out of the room.

Mr. Prentice sighed as he watched him go and Lottie Spate looked up, a little surprised at the hurried departure.

"What should one do?" Mr. Prentice asked the dog. "A woman buys a house in a quiet court and, without any encouragement from her, first Mr. Speed falls in love with her. He is supplanted by Mr. Cumming; then Mr. Fawcett, ever on the watch to guard the world against the lusts of the flesh and the devil, threatens her with the penalties of hell fire; and falls in love with her himself. Even her affection for the child is murdered by the jealousy of its mother, and the disaffection of her brother. Pursued and tormented by their passions, distracted by the fulminations of the man of God, threatened and finally shorn of all hope of peace, she rushes away to loneliness and death." Mr. Prentice paused and pulled the long ears of the dog gently. "That is what appears on the surface. That is what Mr. Treacher would see if they would let him. But they've closed the ranks because they are afraid; and it is fear that spins the world. They are afraid of two things—the first is obvious, their own behaviour. If the wheeling light of publicity should halt and their tawdry figures be outlined, that would be disastrous for them. But outweighing that fear is another; somehow, in some way, they are vaguely aware there is something esoteric in the whole business. Iris is dead and suddenly the passions subside, and they are left wondering at themselves. What rare air have they breathed? What frenzy seized and shook them? They don't know, but they are uncomfortable, as persons who imagine they are being followed, but when they throw uneasy looks over their shoulders find nothing except their shadows that pop up and pass them as they approach and leave behind the lamp posts."

Markham came in to draw the curtains and Mr. Prentice stopped fondling the dog.

"Lady Iris is dead," Mr. Prentice told him bluntly. "She shot herself."

Markham's hand paused on the curtain.

"When?" he asked.

Mr. Prentice looked at him in some surprise.

"You know I quite forgot to ask Mr. Treacher that," he replied. "But perhaps that was because I knew," he muttered to himself.

"Then I hope we get some peace," Markham said, drawing the curtains together vigorously. "This house needs it." He looked at Mr. Prentice uneasily. "You don't think she will——"

"No, I don't," Mr. Prentice interrupted him sharply.

"She was a very unhappy woman," Markham said.

"How do you know?" Mr. Prentice asked.

"I heard her crying," Markham answered. "That's why I wouldn't sleep in the house alone," he went on defiantly.

"Nonsense; that was the child across the way or perhaps Mrs. Cumming," Mr. Prentice said. "Which reminds me I've never thanked Violette for her mother's picture," he added inconsequently, "and for——" He stopped and threw an affectionate glance towards it where it stood in the centre of the mantelpiece.

"Violette!" Markham exclaimed with a sniff.

"I shall call on her after dinner," Mr. Prentice said with unwonted decision. "I expect she'll be lonely," he added, more to himself than to Markham. "I suppose you won't mind being left by yourself?" he asked him in a louder voice.

"Whatever it was seems to have gone," Markham answered slowly. "Do you mean to say you've noticed nothing since we've been here?"

"I never said I hadn't," Mr. Prentice replied evasively. "But when people live alone as you and I have done for so many years, I think they are apt to become hypersensitive."

Markham considered this.

"Maybe," he admitted. "Anyway, you needn't think I am going to leave you because I'm not."

Giving Mr. Prentice a curious look of mingled defiance and sorrow, he closed the door behind him very carefully; and Mr. Prentice knew that that was as far as he would ever get in unravelling the skein of his servant's thoughts and conclusions.

In honour of his forthcoming call on Mrs. Dawson Mr. Prentice took great pains with his toilet; at least, that was the reason for his dawdling which he put forward to himself and did not trouble to deny. What he was really trying to do, however, was to keep his mind occupied so that he might avoid any journey in retrospect. In some way, for some reason, it seemed to him that he had found himself caught up in the infinite and had touched the unsubstantial hem of the garment of eternal verity. Was there a purpose behind all this? Or had he accidentally put his finger upon the mysterious combination of sign and symbol that gave him for an instant a glimpse into the safe which held the mainspring of the universe?

"'Beauty is truth, truth beauty—and that is all ye know on earth and all ye need to know.'" He found himself turning over the well-known lines in his mind when he crossed the courtyard to pay his call on Mrs. Dawson. It never occurred to him that she might be out; it never occurred to him because there appeared to him to be an inevitability about this segment of his existence; and there was just one tiny piece of the centre of the pattern that was a little faded, a fraction out of focus. He rang the bell, the light sprang up in the iron lantern and Mrs. Dawson opened the door. She looked a little surprised.

"I wasn't expecting you," she said. "But come in. Toddy isn't here." She paused. "Of course, you've heard the news," she went on.

Mr. Prentice nodded and she led the way into the sitting-room.

"I came to thank you for the picture of your mother," he said. "It was a very kind thought on your part."

"You were kind to me," she answered. "Toddy told me the other thing had come off too."

"And to thank you for that as well," Mr. Prentice continued. "You are really being very good to me."

"I have a soft heart for men with illusions," Mrs. Dawson replied lightly. "As a rule they are so hopelessly impractical themselves that something has to be done to subsidize them. I don't want you to have to move from here for lack of cash. Did that detective fellow come and bother you?" She switched the subject, but was careful to keep her voice cool and nonchalant.

"Yes, he came in a couple of times," Mr. Prentice answered equally flatly.

"So she's dead," Mrs. Dawson went on a little less brittlely. "And that will be the end of a lot of things—including, I suspect, your curiosity. Do you know why she died?"

Mr. Prentice nodded.

"Oh yes," he answered.

"Care to tell me?"

Mr. Prentice looked at her in silence a moment.

"She died," he said at length, "because she had delivered her message."

Mrs. Dawson stared at him in frank bewilderment.

"I haven't the least idea what you're talking about," she replied.

Mr. Prentice smiled at her; it was a benign smile that held in it no seeds of superiority.

"The police," he went on, "are anxious to find out the state of her mind at the time. I can tell them that. Even Markham knew she was very sad."

"But neither you nor Markham ever met her so far as I know," Mrs. Dawson objected.

"If you mean in the conventional fashion you are perfectly right," Mr. Prentice agreed, "but you don't have to shake hands with people in order to meet them. Many people see the snowdrop, but how many hear, like Schumann, its bell heralding the spring? One can walk into a person's house and from that house one can deduce a great deal. Someone once said, 'Show me a man's library and I will tell you what manner of man he is.' Markham was convinced he heard her crying and he was afraid. I don't know why he thought she was crying, but I also saw her crying out in the courtyard by the marigolds—and I think I know."

"You saw her!"

"Figuratively speaking. I now suspect it was a very vivid dream," Mr. Prentice answered blandly. "You may not know it, but the marigold is the flower of the Virgin Mary and Iris was weeping, but not for her own misfortune. That she was sorry for herself is what the police will deduce if they ever get hold of the story, which I very much doubt. She did not commit suicide because she was driven to it by the importunity of the men or the unkindness of the women— and that may relieve your mind somewhat. That is only the picture you are meant to see. No," he went on gently, "that is only the surface of the tragedy." He paused and then continued in the easy conversational tones of a man instructing a favourite pupil. "One of the daughters of Oceanus, my dear Violette," he continued, "was named Iris. She was the especial messenger of Hera. She was a Virgin Goddess; she was also the bringer of discord and her path between heaven and earth is marked by the rainbow. Now Lady Iris was born in 1914," he smiled at her gravely, "and you will admit there has been turmoil ever since."

"She was Toddy's sister," Mrs. Dawson put in flatly.

"But was she? I gathered when I was up at the Hall that Lord Rawton had no intention of acknowledging her and probably would not have done so if his wife hadn't died in childbirth. She had also a very curious room—I occupied it—and a still more curious picture—I saw it. There were the wings and the caduceus—the herald's staff, you know. And she was always travelling."

"This is a fairy story for Paula," Mrs. Dawson said with good-natured contempt.

"She told Paula a good many stories," Mr. Prentice reminded her, "and you did not like them. They may have been myths to you, but they were real to her. She had a message to give; and she has taken a long time to give it, and she wept not for self-pity, but for the world."

"What are you trying to tell me?" Mrs. Dawson asked.

Mr. Prentice rose to his feet and stood in front of her, a

rotund figure in his striped trousers and black jacket, but at the moment not without a touch of dignity.

"I am trying to let you have a glimpse of the pattern that is so elusive," he said, raising his voice. "The civilized world destroyed the ancient myths and the Gods have sent down their messenger. She has seen the world as it is to-day and among the marigolds, one of the flowers of Christianity, she weeps for it. I am asking you what you have gained and what you have lost. Where is beauty and where have you hidden truth? I am asking you whether you have not substituted one myth for another to lose the golden age and the happiness of mankind. I am asking——"

Mr. Prentice was halted in full flight by the slow opening of the door and his features, which had grown set and stern, relaxed as he saw Paula standing in the doorway, her thumb stuck in her mouth, her fair curls scattered and her blue eyes very widely awake.

"I heard voices," she said.

"You must go back to bed, dear," her mother commanded, a little agitated under the lash of Mr. Prentice's tongue.

"Not just yet," Mr. Prentice pleaded. "Tell me, Paula— you know now that Iris won't be coming back?"

Paula nodded.

"Yes," she answered in a rush of words. "She told me if I saw a rainbow—and I'd never seen one then—she told me all about it—if I saw it she said I'd know she'd gone back to her real home."

"And did she tell you anything else?" Mr. Prentice asked eagerly. "Did she give you a message of any kind?"

Paula looked at him gravely for a long time; she opened her mouth to speak and then she suddenly laughed. Mr. Prentice was taken aback.

"What is so funny, dear?" her mother asked her.

"He looks like a penguin, a fat one," she replied.

Mrs. Dawson smiled.

"I don't think fat is a very nice word," she objected. looking at Mr. Prentice with affectionate good humour. "Portly, perhaps."

Mr. Prentice sighed and turned away towards the door.

"I don't think I am quite as stupid as a penguin," he said. "But," he went on to Paula, "you can call me a peregrine, if you like. The portly peregrine."

"What's a peregrine?" her mother asked for her.

"A peregrine in my case is a man who is outside the territory of the ancient world; and therefore away from home," he answered. "We shall know, all in good time, what message Iris gave to you," he said to Paula as he laid his hand lightly on her fair head. "Nothing is certain, is it?"

"Nothing is certain, is it?" she repeated. "That is the great thing about life. You told me that."

With the echo of his own words in his ears Mr. Prentice stepped once more into the courtyard, wondering to whom the Gods had chosen to give victory in the fateful years to come which were the heritage of Paula.

Books by Peter Traill

THE DECEIVING MIRROR

"Recommended thriller, skilfully carpentered by a novelist who really knows his business. Plenty of sound psychological stuffing to make the story plausible." *Daily Mail*.

"One of the rare detective-stories in which the motive is adequate and the crime and its perpetrator fit with a click. Unsuspected depths of baseness are dramatically revealed. There is much art in the telling and intermittent skill in the characterisation." *The Sketch*.

MIDNIGHT OIL

This is the fourth volume of Peter Traill's *short stories to be published; here are what the critics think of the other three:*

"Mr. Peter Traill pursues his irresistible way. His stories are brisk, compact, and complete—sometimes a perfect gem of plot and exploitation." *Manchester Guardian*.

"Mr. Traill's stories are all, or nearly all, conceived in a spirit of delicate irony. Sometimes the irony is light, sometimes the note deepens, but the treatment is invariably good." *The Scotsman*.

Books by Peter Traill

THE WEDDING OF THE JACKAL

Sunday Mercury: "A lightsome, satirical treatise on love . . . highly amusing." *Tatler:* "Gay, light, teasing. . . ." *Observer:* "Practised skill and wit."

NO FARTHING RICHER

Manchester Daily Dispatch: "Gay with nonsense and light humour. There is many a laugh in this book." *Yorkshire Evening News:* "Mr. Traill's stories are light fantasy spun around the curious character of Mr. Cribbage, who is that rare thing, a funny character who is funny."

UNDER THE PLANE TREES

Further delightful London episodes in the career of the urbane, cultured and witty Mr. Cribbage. A clever sophisticated volume in the same inimitable vein of its predecessors.